Answers in Simulation

Iurii Vovchenko

PART 1

Hell.

"Science cannot solve the ultimate mystery of nature. And that is because, in the last analysis, we ourselves are a part of the mystery that we are trying to solve."

Max Planck

1

AMAZING

Robbie was sitting on his favorite bench in Kinnear Park, enjoying the warm April sun. He was watching ants scouting the area around a soda can, dropped by someone who probably didn't care to do a few extra steps to put the trash in a garbage can. However, this time, Robbie was grateful to that stranger as he enjoyed watching ants rumbling around the can searching for sugar. One of the ants was sipping soda nectar from a large drop on the can's top. Robbie imagined a smile on the ant's face as the little guy was eating all that sugar. "Ants cannot smile, " thought Robbie. He remembered Dreamwork's Antz movie. He was a little boy when that came out. He was captivated by how much drama animators created around the tiny insects: uprising, friendship, love. "Ants cannot do that, only humans can, " thought Robbie now.

One of the ants, near the bottom of the can, was floating motionless in a drop of soda. Robbie didn't feel sorry for the dead insect. The insect suffocated enjoying the tasty treat, and while dying, it didn't realize what was happening to it. Robbie's thoughts turned to Frederick the Great, who ruled Prussia in the Eighteenth century. Robbie read a book about the guy; and what an amazing person he was. Prussia was at the Seven Years' War surrounded by the enemy coalition from all sides. Yet he fought all of them with firm resolve, risking his life many times in many battles, not letting desperation or fear overcome him. He didn't allow the enemies to grab any land in exchange for him staying in power and saving his life. He was victorious in the end, and Prussia didn't lose any territory. "It is easy to die if you don't know what death even means..." thought Robbie.

Robbie turned his attention to the clouds. Today, they were absolutely beautiful, bright shades of white, cheerful and fast. He was admiring them for a few minutes and quickly got bored.

Robbie looked at the ant on the top of the can. "He is the ants champion, the alpha male," Robbie chuckled. He observed the ant closely; the creature looked ugly: tiny black dots for the eyes and scary looking tentacles, continually moving and sensing the environment. "Yeah, ants in Antz had big eyes and could smile and talk. That has nothing in common with real ants. It seems whatever movie they make, the main characters always have human traits. Are we even able to make a story about something that doesn't have human traits?" Robbie wondered. "How about a story of a real cloud would look like? Here I am. A bunch of water vapor traveling the skies," Robbie chuckled again.

Robbie worked as a technical writer for one of Seattle's big software companies. The job paid well, but like many jobs-that-pay-well, it was not his passion. He had to produce detailed and intuitive instructions for the users. Click here, press there, then you see this.

Robbie worked with Scott, a senior technical writer. Scott truly loved his job, and Robbie was envious. Scott did the exact same work as Robbie, except he did it with passion. Scott would bug every software developer and product manager until he produced a perfect help file. Scott bragged once, "I always hated to unbox products and read instructions that are hard to follow, so I made it my objective to be the best at instructions. I can write a script for a nuclear power plant, which can be followed even by a 5-year-old". "OK, Scott, you are great. I wonder if people like you exist in the hotel cleaning business," thought Robbie sarcastically, as he genuinely was irritated by Scott's passion for an ordinary job like theirs. Robbie wanted to believe that Scott was simply showing off and pretended to be in love with his career just to get promoted.

Scott, like Robbie, was a dark-haired male of average height in his late 20s. "Scott and I probably look so similar to the cloud from up there. Yet we are so different. I guess that doesn't apply to the ants that much. They are just little clones of each other," thought Robbie.

More ants were coming in. The scouts finished their job, and worker ants were building trails to bring food to the nest. Ant soldiers rambled around protecting the workers. This scene reminded Robbie of the company he worked for, "I guess humans are also good at building hierarchies and assigning responsibilities. I do the scripts and online help files. We have developers making software and test engineers testing it. We have product managers responsible for the product ultimate look and feel. We have marketing and sales. Everybody knows what he needs to do. Together we can do a lot. Ants build their skyscrapers underground while we built our tower downtown, and Seattle itself is our park."

Charlie woke up and reluctantly hit the soda can with his brown paw. The ants flew in all directions disappearing in the grass. They would live, just couldn't be observed anymore.

Charlie was a twelve-year-old Labrador. Great dog. "Charlie loves Robbie," everybody said. Charlie was getting old. Now he slept most of the time even when being in the park. "Scientists say that dogs can't smile, but dogs can express happiness and anger probably much better than humans. What are the other emotions out there?" Robbie wondered. He tried to remember other emotions," Sadness, joy, surprise, and fear. Dogs can do all of those! How far are humans from dogs? Are dogs like 97% human and ants 2% human? Can you measure that? Are humans 33% of God?"

Robbie noticed a homeless person passing by. The person was shaking, and he looked like one of the worst types of homeless. The poor guy was mad and possessed by anger, cursing at someone invisible. The smell of urination and decay filled the air. The madman noticed the soda can and picked it up, trying to drink anything left inside. "He must be 20% of Charlie," thought Robbie. The thought of even trying to compare the two hurt. "Should we allow to compare life? Yes, Scott is better at work, but I love Charlie, and the dog lived a happy life with me. Maybe before meth kicked in this homeless being was someone's handsome, smart, and kind child? Back then he was maybe better than Charlie?" the comparison thought continued to drill through Robbie, "So if a human can decrease his percent by living the bad life, maybe he can increase it too by living the good one? Can animals be in control of their percent too?"

The homeless person took a few desperate sips from the soda can. After making sure it was completely empty, he slowly walked to the garbage can, bashing all the Gods who were to blame for his misery and threw the can into the trash. He looked further down the park trail, something left near a linden tree attracted his attention, and he continued his usual evening stroll.

Robbie was surprised. The homeless person threw the garbage into the trash as if he was concerned with the park's tidiness. "Would Charlie bring trash to a garbage can if not trained to do so? Would Charlie do anything just because it is Good?" Robbie was not sure anymore if his "20% of Charlie" estimate was right. Robbie remembered his Sunday school. "Man is created in the image of God and can tell Good from Evil. Unlike animals. Sure! Here we go," smirked Robbie. He was brought up protestant Christian, but gave up on that in his early 20s, like many others at that age.

Robbie remembered Nadarkhani story, a Christian pastor in

Iran, who was sentenced to death for apostasy. Nadarkhani was offered a choice to convert to Islam and save his life or face a death sentence. He chose to die. Robbie, being a science guy, and self-proclaimed agnostic was fascinated by such a choice made by a middle-aged, well to do, totally sane family man. He had often seen people doing crazy dangerous things in the news and in internet videos. They were risking their lives for no apparent reason. All those were qualified as either professional, insane, young and stupid, or just intoxicated ones. Nadarkhani did it for a different reason, he was 'jumping off the cliff' for something significant deep down in his soul.

Anne was quickly approaching Robbie's bench. As she was jogging, a couple of doves that were eating crumbs at the center of the paved trail got disturbed by her steps. Instead of flying off, the lazy birds simply cleared the middle of the trail and waited on the side letting her pass. As she passed, they quickly returned to their central position loudly complaining about the disturbance. Anne stopped near Robbie and said, catching her breath, "Hi guys. Nice and warm today, isn't it?". Robbie smiled and said, "Yeah. Perfect. No wind or rain either." "Well, enjoy!" she chirped. Anne patted Charlie and continued her usual jogging routine. Anne was pretty and young, a happy girl. Everyone liked her and wanted to be her friend. She would often stop and pat Charlie or talk about recent news. Robbie liked her a lot. Even without really knowing her, he could see that she was a kind and caring person. Robbie had the talent to see through people and emotionally feel them. Was Anne the reason he came to Kinnear Park instead of much closer located Queen Anne Greenbelt?

Robbie looked at disappearing Anne's silhouette. "Maybe if I start jogging with her, we can get to know each other better?" Robbie thought. Anne stopped to say a few words to another jogger, a tall man in his late 30s, a manager type. "She is so beautiful, and I am just an average guy, she meets a hundred like me every day. If I were someone like that guy or even better, a famous scientist like Einstein, then I would stand a chance," Robbie dreamed. The thought of Einstein being a playboy made Robbie smile. He remembered many famous people in history: Hemingway, Newton, Bach, Tsiolkovsky and many others. They formed what humanity knew and how people thought today. They changed everything by just being humans. Humans were amazing.

The sunset time was approaching. People loved Kinnear Park for its picturesque view of Elliot Bay, which was especially peaceful and calming during sunset. Unfortunately, the park was considered unsafe after dark. It was time for Robbie to go, but not because of the safety. He didn't like sunsets, they reminded him of the imminent end of life. Robbie prepared to leave. He looked at Charlie, who was staring somewhere far away into the Bay. Charlie looked sad. Was he thinking about the end of life too?

Robbie picked up his backpack and stood up. Charlie's mood changed suddenly, he was wagging his tail in anticipation of a warm meal at home, which he always had together with his owner after every evening walk.

2

ROBBIE

Robbie's father was a lumber mill manager in Redmond. In 2001 the mill went bankrupt, and he struggled to find a better job for four years since then. Random short stints were interrupted by periods of doing nothing. Binge-watching TV and drinking occupied most of his days. He died when Robbie was 16. Probably the worst age to lose a father.

The most defining memory of his father for Robbie was the week before his father passed away. They talked about whether it is better to do hiking or fishing as a father-son leisure activity. They never did either. In-fact their father-son activities usually happened in front of a TV, as they loved discussing the latest news and making fun of talking heads. They decided to try hiking first and then try fishing to see what goes better. They were making plans for the next weekend. Then he died next Friday from a blood clot causing a severe stroke. Doctors suspected chronic alcoholism as the probable cause.

Robbie loved his father. Even though dad was drinking heavily and suffered from depression, he stayed a loving and caring parent. They always had topics to talk about. Father would often blame globalization and big software companies making Redmond a different place. He longed for a simpler life. He dreamed about old times and how they could happily live on a farm in the Midwest. Robbie and his father spent a lot of time in the backyard doing woodwork projects. Robbie's father loved to work with wood. He made most of the home furniture himself. Robbie often helped him, and once Robbie made a stool for his father's birthday. Dad kept that stool for himself and always used it when having breakfast. Would Robbie want a better father? He would not.

Robbie's mother had to support the family after dad lost his job. She was a day-to-day fighter like so many women are. She worked hard at her day job as a quality control engineer and then she had to look after the house, look after Robbie, and look after Robbie's father who often was in a state providing no opportunity of getting from point A to point B in the house without someone helping him. She was very strict with Robbie, very strict with Robbie's father. She would often scream at both, and they would slowly obey her command, as there was no option not to obey.

Robbie was afraid of his mother. Sometimes she would bust in long and loud angry monologues about small things, like unwashed dishes or forgetting to close the entrance door. Robbie had to hide in his room to escape those and stay there until she cooled off. She often slapped Robbie. As Robbie grew older, he learned to ignore her anger. In his late teens, he became bigger than her physically and had his own strong opinions about things. She stopped touching him, and she grew more ignorant of his presence.

Robbie had no idea what to do with his life. He was on autopilot mode. He had straight As in school, but he really didn't participate in anything outside regular school classes. Dad took "go figure it out yourself" stance, and mom didn't have time or energy to push Robbie in any specific direction. Robbie had no brothers or sisters and didn't have many close friends either. Most of his time was spent on computer games and reading books. He loved reading. In 2004, the same year when Robbie's dad died, father gave Robbie Sony Librie for birthday. It was the first e-reader device on the market, way before Kindle. Father told him, "Read as much as you can. This is the only way to really get what this world is about." Then father told him how Robbie's granddad had a library and father being a boy himself at the time would read all those books. And how that helped him to get the lumber mill manager job. So Robbie was reading. He would download anything he could get on the device. It was hard to get electronic books back then, and Robbie was scouting the internet for books to download. Later he bought a Kindle and read, even more, every evening, just before falling asleep.

Robbie was never interested in money. They lived well. Even when Robbie's father was unemployed and was drinking, they still lived well and could afford good food and clothes, entertainment, and vacations, like any other middle-class families. Money saved during father's mill manager job helped a lot. In 2008 Robbie quickly got into local DigiPen, picking arts as his major. He picked arts as it seemed the easiest major to graduate in. He continued to live with mom. Mom agreed to pay his tuition if Robbie continued to live with her and work part-time. So Robbie was lucky and avoided getting into student debt. He enjoyed the walks to the campus right from his house. Robbie worked as a freelance writer for various magazines. It was easy living.

Robbie spent most of his time doing classes, reading books and playing computer games. Nothing changed for him after leaving high school and starting university. During the Great Recession, mom lost her quality engineer job. She was a real fighter though. Robbie never saw mom cry, not now, not even when his father died. She quickly got a warehouse job doing night shifts.

Robbie didn't notice the 'change'. Though the 'change' was happening anyway. People have no control of the 'change', they can only anticipate it, contemplate it, and react to it. In the 90s mom was driving a new BMW E39. In 2000s she was driving a new 2002 Toyota Camry. In 2012, the year Robbie was graduating, she was still driving the same 2002 Toyota Camry. Robbie had his father's old Honda Civic and was happy with it.

After graduation, Robbie couldn't find a day job. The year 2012 was a tough year for employment, but Robbie didn't try hard either. After a few 'We will call you' he gave up and continued making pennies on his freelancing. Robbie was still not sure what he wanted to do in life. He was definitely not ready to start a family. He was not excited about dating either. The only dating experience he had was a girl he met at Comic-Con gaming convention. They dated for three months, but something didn't work out, and she just said Robbie was not the right fit for her. Robbie didn't know what the real reason was. He liked girls, but he had no clue how to approach girls or what to talk about with them. He enjoyed being with the Comic Con girl, they had a great trip to Montana, but after the trip, the relationship went sour by the day. They often were sitting quietly, not knowing what to talk about. Robbie could predict what her reply would be to his questions, and she could probably do the same.

Robbie's social life was his gaming buddies. They played the World of Guns online and met every Friday night at Tom's place. Tom Colton was the leader of their team. One day Robbie returned home from Tom's and saw mom lying on a sofa. She was smoking. The only time he saw mom smoke was when he was 15; mom and his father just had a happy date night in the city, they parked their car near the neighbor's house; they talked about something and laughed.

Mom got up off the sofa and looked at Robbie with a sad and alien look. "How was your game meeting?" she asked, trying to smile and hide the cigarette. "It was usual," Robbie answered. "We are losing our home," she said coldly. Then she began weeping. Robbie noticed wrinkles on her face that he never noticed before. Robbie came to mom and hugged her; he gently patted her head. He noticed patches of gray hair that he didn't see before either. Mom stopped weeping as suddenly as she began. "Do you want me to rent a one-bedroom or two-bedroom?" she asked. "One-bedroom," answered Robbie.

Tom was a software developer in one of the largest companies in Seattle. He learned about the house situation from Robbie and suggested to apply for the technical writer opening that was recently posted at his workplace. Robbie applied and got his first full-time job. He was surprised at how easy it was to get. Probably his sizable freelance portfolio helped. He rented a decent place in Seattle's West Queen Anne neighborhood while Mom moved to a rental close to her warehouse job. Robbie visited mom every second month. It was all good again.

Robbie was fine.

3

WORLD OF GAMES

Four young, fit, unmarried, well to do, modern-day heroes had a pleasant evening in the downtown Seattle apartment.

"I'm God!" Tom said with a great sense of pride.

"My Mod lets you remotely control zombies, creepers, and skeletons, like in a chess game. In Cubecraft game, those are the most numerous monsters," Tom continued.

"Super Cool," enthusiastically said Martin, "Are you going to make money off it?"

"Nah," said Tom, "It's all free. In fact, I lose money on hosting that. I do that mostly for fun."

"At your age, it is time to do something for money," said Martin with a smirk.

"Well, at least I do something that people like. I enjoy it too. Money is not everything. Moreover, money won't matter much very soon. Haven't you heard of automation and robots? We'll all just get a universal income and be busy creating stuff for fun. Soon, I think, money won't even be around as we'll get everything for free. Energy will be free from the sun, and robots will manufacture, grow, and deliver everything else," said Tom with even more pride in his voice.

"I guess Karl Marx was right after all," Robbie laughed.

"Games are the future of everything. People won't need to go to work. How do you think they'll spend their time? I can understand you can have more fun in Hawaii, but here, in gloomy Seattle, people will just stay at home and play games 24/7," Tom continued his futuristic vision.

"Anyways, let's discuss our Himmelsdorf map strategy again. Martin, you should switch from playing artillery to a light tank. I know you don't like playing anything but SPG, but that map is just not SPG friendly. All action happens in the city streets. We need another tank player, not SPG," suggested Tom.

"My whole life, I played snipers, gunners, or archers. I like fighting from a safe distance. Sorry but playing for a tank is out of the question," answered Martin with resolve.

"Yeah, everyone knows you are a camper, Martin... Then Robbie will have to switch to a heavy tank to give us more overall tank power," decided Tom with irritation.

"I'm fine with heavies," said Robbie, taking a sip of his lager beer.

"Good. And Alex will play his usual scouting tactic," suggested Tom, turning to Alex with optimism. Alex was already asleep on the sofa.

"I guess it is time to wrap this up, gentlemen," said Tom with all seriousness as if he was resolving the Cuban missile crisis. Martin woke up Alex, and they quickly left.

Robbie was not in a rush. He was drinking his beer, waiting for Tom to close the door after Martin and Alex. "Can you show me your Cubecraft game Mod?" asked Robbie.

"Sure," answered Tom.

Tom showed Robbie his Mod. He explained that he could control any block's look, motion, and properties via scripting in Cubecraft's virtual world. Robbie knew that it was Tom's favorite topic. Tom, as usual, switched his attention to making analogies between the real world and Cubecraft's world. He suggested that just like Cubecraft, our world could also be just a simulation, and instead of Cubecraft's building blocks, our universe is built with simulated atoms and photons and such. He said that people got it all wrong with humans being just connected to the virtual world and instead humans themselves and their brain function is only simulated electrochemical reactions between virtual elemental particles. There were no humans anywhere but in the simulation, according to Tom.

"There is no soul, just simulated neurons in a virtual brain," exclaimed Tom with confidence.

"You'll need a pretty big computer to simulate every atom and photon and every interaction among them," said Robbie, trying to convert the number of atoms in the universe to the number of transistors such a computer would need.

"Size doesn't matter!" answered Tom with irritation, "And when you die, you're just erased from memory," said Tom viciously, sort of punishing Robbie in his mind for the sarcastic question.

"OK, I better be going. Charlie is probably nervous by now," said Robbie, finishing his beer. Robbie quickly left Tom's place.

After a short drive, Robbie parked the car at his reserved parking spot. He climbed the stairs to the second floor and opened the door. Charlie was at the porch, always happy to see his kind master. They ate the night snack together, and both went to sleep.

Robbie couldn't fall asleep that night. He felt energized and full of ideas after the meeting. He was trying to imagine a computer owner who would run a whole human known universe simulation on a computer. "Could be a geek like Tom or me, playing God, only his computer trillions of times more powerful," Robbie chuckled. "Or maybe crazy scientists doing some evil experiments on us? Or maybe, like in Truman show, we are just a popular TV 24/7 program among aliens? Maybe I am the star?" Robbie chuckled again.

Robbie remembered the popular Sims game. He liked to play it when he was younger. He also remembered the Islanders game, which he played just a year ago. "Humans really like to care for their little Minions. Humans enjoy being Gods. Sheep and their Shepherd caring for them," a thought flashed through Robbie's mind. The word "care" had a close connection with the Bible for Robbie; he read the whole book in his teens. "Maybe the Bible was right after all. Our computer-owner-God cares about us, and we are just his little Tamagotchies?" He remembered The Legend of Zelda quest game. "Quest games always have those little puzzles and hints. Maybe the Bible is a hint placed by God so we can successfully win the "life" game? Who is smart now. All Christians will be saved indeed!" the thought made Robbie feel a little bit uneasy.

Robbie finally felt tired. His eyes closed. "Most games have a script that you are supposed to follow, I hope our "life" game is free-for-all open-world one," thought Robbie slowly falling asleep. He dreamed of Anne and him building a house in the Cubecraft world.

4

THE ANT NEST

Robbie took his usual bike ride to the headquarters. He wore a purple pullover and jeans, which didn't help much against the cold morning rain. Robbie loved bike rides, except for the days like this, which for Seattle was more a rule than an exception. "I would definitely be better off in LA weather," he thought. Robbie many times considered moving to the Southwest, but every time he was able to find a ton of reasons against the move: too expensive, too hot in summer, hard to find a new job, and, of course, those California fires.

He stopped in front of a tall glass tower. Leaving the bike behind, he entered the main entrance with dozens of others ahead and behind him. It was the beginning of another working day.

Exiting the elevator, Robbie got to his place by making precisely 10 steps. Scott was not at his desk yet, which was unusual. Martin's loud voice was heard throughout the vast open office space. The rows of long tables reminded Robbie of the Oktoberfest, except the tables had laptops and not beer on them. Martin was always first in the office, so he could overlap with the teams across the ocean. Martin was a product manager in Robbie's team. It was declared as a non-management role; he was kind of manager anyways. Martin was a self-proclaimed people connector and a problem solver. He also loved computer games, as that what helped him, in his own words "let guano out." People mostly didn't like him for being the noisiest guy on the floor. Martin usually wore glasses and a smart business suit at work. Everyone in the office knew that Martin had good eyesight. He wore glasses just to look smart. Martin was also famous for trying new things first. He was the first in the office to use a smartwatch and camera glasses. Robbie was not close to Martin, but they were getting along. In fact, Robbie couldn't name a person he wouldn't get along with.

Tom came out of the elevator and went straight to his place without looking around. He had the famous t-shirt on him with his name in binary code. Tom had gray shorts despite cold rain. He got into coding right away. He was fixated at the current problem to solve and didn't see anything around himself. There was something robotic about Tom. "No surprise he likes to think that he lives in a computer simulation. Only robots would enjoy such an idea," chuckled Robbie.

The last to arrive of the World of Guns brigade was Alex. He came out of the elevator, waved to Robbie and went straight to the canteen. He was about to get himself an excellent free morning coffee with a free donut, probably his primary motivation to come to the office in the mornings. Alex was wearing a green polo shirt with a small hydrogen atom imprint. He had brown khakis and a pair of slip-on shoes. He suddenly stopped next to the office's glass wall. The wall was intended for creative drawing, which was in line with the modern office fashion. He drew a tank with a smiley face and blinked to

Robbie. Then he continued his route to the canteen. Alex was a software tester converted from a Ph.D. Physicist. He explained that his particle physics Ph.D. job was a dead end and that he was tired of fighting for grants, while his pay was miserable. With the software testing job, he was getting more money for the same effort. Alex always liked to emphasize the "effort" part of the sentence. Alex was especially close to Martin.

Scott was unusually late today. In fact, he was never late. Robbie spent most of the working days with Scott. Scott was one of the guys who interviewed him and played a crucial part in hiring him. Scott helped Robbie get up-to-speed with the job. Scott was a self-driven individual, with a sort of black and white vision of the world. He often pushed Robbie too much without offering any help. Scott often said, "You have to do it yourself, Robbie, to really get how it should be done. I am not sharing my work with you." Robbie thought of Scott as Ayn Rand's Henry Rearden character, only without money, and without good looks. Robbie was irritated by Scott's very active work style. "Why can't he just do his help files quietly for eight hours and leave to home? He is not a CEO or something to run around the office like that," Robbie thought. Scott and Martin were the old-timers on the floor; everyone respected them.

Robbie preferred to work completely alone, but that was against the company's team-centric philosophy. "What is this crazy obsession with the team being everything and individual nothing? I thought we live in a capitalistic country, yet large corporations make individuals feel like nothing as if we live in Stalinist Russia. Is this a new economic system? Probably should be called Commie Capitalism" thought Robbie appreciating his wit.

The company, Robbie worked for was a fantastic success. The early employees were millionaires by now. Some people worked here for years doing very little actual work and getting a lot of money. Robbie had a secret plan to become one of those. It was easy for a lazy but smart person to hide in the thousands of other troops. Robbie felt sorry for his father, who worked long hours at his mill making the same money as some recent young graduates here. "Is it fair?" thought Robbie "Why market economy doesn't do what it is supposed to do – self regulate. Reward the hard-working and punish lazy ones."

Robbie didn't consider himself lazy. When he was a freelancer, he did some of the projects for 15 hours non stop. Of course, if they were interesting enough to him. He didn't consider himself an 8-5 person. Robbie always had a sense that he needed to do something special. He just didn't know what that 'something special' was.

The elevator door opened, and Scott came out slowly. He got to his place, saying 'hi' to Robbie without looking. Scott had a pitch-black turtleneck with the Yin and Yang symbol on the back. Scott always wore dark turtlenecks with jeans for work. Everyone giggled behind his back, considering him as another one of Steve Jobs admirers. "Bad morning?" asked Robbie. Scott turned to Robbie; he looked at Robbie, yet it felt like he didn't see him. "Yeah, sort of" replied Scott with some tension. After a pause, Scott's eyes finally focused on Robbie, and he smiled. "It is going to be a fun day. We will be sending our work to all 34 translators. Get ready for lots of questions in all accents imaginable." he cheered his associate.

Robbie didn't have fun. It was exhausting for him to answer the same questions over and over again from all the translators while checking the time every twenty minutes hoping to get to 5pm somehow. The canteen was a big help. He had enough coffee already by now, and his head felt the overload. "Even coffee doesn't help me anymore to live through the day," he thought. He decided to take a "resort break." Robbie would go to the restroom, lock the stall, and sit there for a while, watching funny videos on his phone. It was a popular way to let the day go, and not just for Robbie. Very often all stalls were taken for the same reason. That happened today as well. Unwilling to wait, he returned to his place. "Oh, why we need to suffer so much in the 21st century!" he screamed in his mind, "We are humans! The rulers of this planet, and we should just enjoy every moment that we have."

At last, it was 5pm on the clock. Robbie quickly escaped the building and had his uneventful ride back home. Charlie was happy to see his master. They had another calm and cozy evening together. Yet Robbie knew that tomorrow he would be suffering the same fate as today.

5

LIFEPLAYING

Robbie enjoyed his usual walk in Kinnear park. Though Charlie was not happy. The light rain made him shiver, and he was uttering quiet woofs every minute or two to emphasize his dissatisfaction with the situation. Robbie was passing the homeless camp. Two poor guys were visibly cold. "Why did they chose to live here? Why don't they move to the south? It would be more comfortable to live outdoors somewhere in LA. They have no home, no job, no family, so they have the luxury to pick any place in the world to live. Yet they picked cold and rainy Seattle," thought Robbie.

Robbie continued past the camp when he saw a group of volunteers giving off food and hot drinks. One member of the group saw Robbie and ran towards him. As he got closer, Robbie recognized Martin's fake glasses.

"Hey, I didn't know that you volunteer," said Robbie with surprise.

"These poor people need help and who if not me," Martin said with traits of sarcasm, "Look how pretty those two volunteer girls are. I'm really after the girls here. It is the best way to get a quality date. The girls have that caring gene in them, always crowding around the needy," he smiled.

"You should try church for even better-quality material," Robbie attempted to make a joke.

"I do go to church occasionally," said Martin," I go for a different reason though. You see, I am not sure if He exists, but if He does... The church is a perfect place for me to find some time and talk to God. You know, just in case. Moreover, if you pick the right day of the month, you can get free coffee and cakes!"

"I thought in Christianity 'Just in case' doesn't work. Were you successful finding a date with these methods?" asked Robbie sarcastically.

"Not yet. I will. Soon. I know. I am working the probability here. Just be patient," said Martin.

"Working the probability?" asked Robbie.

"Yes. There is a certain probability that I meet a girl that will like me in the church. Another probability exists if I meet a girl in the homeless aid group. I just need to keep doing both until just by chance I meet the right girl. Increase the exposure so to speak. I go to yoga class too. I had a lot of success there. Don't laugh," said Martin.

Robbie laughed. A pretty volunteer girl came to Martin and asked him to fold the table that she finished cleaning. Martin told her that he was coming; he turned to Robbie, smiled and blinked to him. Then he said, "I've moved to a new place at Westlake Park. It has an amazing deck. We'll celebrate tomorrow. Alex and Scott will be there. Do ya wanna come? It all starts at 7pm," asked Martin, ready to leave.

"Sure," answered Robbie.

Martin returned to his group and Robbie continued his walk. Robbie didn't believe in helping the homeless, especially after seeing what they did to the park. He was confident that helping them would bring even more homeless to the park. He remembered "The Great Hunger" book by Cecil Woodham. To Robbie, that book was the depiction of the actual suffering back in the old times, when the poor had no support at all from anyone, and the whole Ireland pretty much had no food left. Hard-working families were dying from hunger. Modern poor seemed to Robbie like pussycats of the real poor of the past. "The poor you will always have," remembered Robbie from the Bible.

The next day came quickly. It was 5pm. Robbie took a shower, put on some random, casual clothes, got into a store for a bottle of wine, and was at Westlake Park place at 7:30pm. The apartment was very spacious. Most people were having fun on the huge deck. Martin was a people person. He loved to have guests, and his new place suited him perfectly.

Martin and Alex were arguing about something when Robbie came in. He joined them, grabbing a beer from the buffet table.

"Thanks for inviting, Martin. Looks like a fun party," said Robbie.

"Hey, Robbie, maybe you can help us. Alex thinks that there are no aliens, cause we never got any radio signals," said Martin.

"First of all, it is not only me who thinks that way but also many others. The main point is that we have trillions of star systems around us, some of which are millions of years older than us. So we should have had, just by chance, some more life forms out there with technology at least as advanced as ours. So why no radio signals so far?" Alex made his point.

"Easy, Alex. Aliens don't reveal themselves cause they don't want us to know that they are here and they are hiding the signals from us," said Martin enthusiastically.

"Oh, Martin. You have no understanding of how radio waves work. You can't really hide them.", said Alex.

"I have to side with Alex. Even if there are some advanced civilizations that don't use radio waves or learned how to hide them, there will be many less advanced civilizations too that use radio waves or used radio waves in the past. We would, for sure, detect those signals by now. Space is totally silent in that sense," Robbie concluded.

"Alright, fine. I agree with you," said Martin.

"Man, you change your convictions so easily!" Alex remarked.

"Given good arguments, I always ready to agree. I choose to follow the winner over standing the ground with the looser. That is why I am a good product manager," said Martin.

"You don't always know if you stand your ground with a winner or loser, " commented Robbie.

Martin continued, ignoring his buddies attacks,"You have to be flexible in life. Everything changes all the time, and you just go with what is hot. I started my career as a DVD sales guy. Can you imagine that? Look, where DVDs are now? Imagine if I stayed in that DVD store; where would I be today? Definitely wouldn't be able to afford this place!"

Martin looked at his silent audience and continued his monologue, "That is why life is fun. I love life for its constantly changing and uncertain nature. I call it Lifeplaying. I play life like a game, and I love to win. You, guys, are gamers, so you know that in every game and even at every level within the same game there is a certain winning strategy. All you need to do in real life is to find the right winning strategy, and you will be golden! For example, we work in a big company. The primary winning strategy in a big company is to be nice to everyone. Lick everyone's butt, so to speak. Just by chance over time one of those butts that you licked will be your boss's boss, and you will be on top. In a small company that would be a poor strategy cause just by chance, it is unlikely someone will be on top of your boss. So you have to be aggressive in a small company. Get noticed! Just make sure you stand your ground for the true cause," said Martin with a smirk.

Robbie felt like a rookie standing next to a professional gamer.

"I recently read a book on shamanism. What an interesting point of view. They ..." Martin suddenly stopped as he noticed a pretty younger girl leaving her friend and aiming for the buffet table. Like a strategic bomber, Martin departed his base and intercepted the girl at the buffet table. He bombed her with his standard set of hookup questions.

6

SCIENCE

After being left alone, Robbie and Alex struggled to continue their conversation. Robbie rarely talked to Alex, and when he did, then it was only for brief work-related matters or World of Guns meetups.

"Is fundamental physics really struggling? It is so weird that you switched to a tester job," Robbie asked, trying to keep the conversation going.

"Absolutely. The theoretical foundations of modern physics were formed decades ago. There was a sort of a boom in physics when those principles found practical uses in energy, space, and manufacturing. Now though, there are way too many theoretical physicists and too little useful and truly 'new' discoveries. After we confirmed Higgs Boson, there was not much left to do for the particle physicists specifically. I was one of that cohort. All I did to get a Ph.D. title is retesting, repackaging, and presenting other people's work. If I were to choose the science field now, I would pick the DNA research. Those guys are pretty much ten years from curing cancer," said Alex.

"I saw a documentary about the effort to unify Einstein's relativistic world and quantum physics. Isn't it a real problem still left to solve?" asked Robbie being genuinely interested.

"Ha! Ha! Ha!" Alex laughed with unhealthy and unexpectedly loud laughter, "People have tried to unify those two theories for decades. The smartest people dedicated their whole lives to achieve that goal. I don't want to waste my one and only life on the search and find out later that the theories are simply not compatible. So far, the attempts to unify only brought crazy math abstractions with a bunch of extra dimensions to our natural three-dimensional world. And if you can't explain something in physics, just invent a new dimension or a new particle with a cool name, like Inflaton, or a cool sounding math abstraction like Black Matter. Ha! Ha! Ha!" laughed Alex with his eyes sparkling with unhealthy excitement.

"Yes. I heard about some of those theories. It is beyond my understanding," said Robbie feeling ashamed, "Why do people think there could be other dimensions? Our world loves symmetry in everything. If there are other dimensions, then those extra dimensions will be symmetrically similar to our current three dimensions. Therefore, we would occasionally see interference from those invisible dimensions, like a house suddenly disappearing or something suddenly appearing. Imagine a two-dimensional sheet of paper, on which a two-dimensional human lives. Then you take a pencil in 3 dimensions and place a dot on the sheet of paper. Now you have a dot in two dimensions that seem to have appeared out of nowhere to that flat human on paper. With the abundance of smartphones, we would see a lot of such 'miracles' from other dimensions in the internet videos by now."

"I haven't thought about it that way," said Alex, a bit perplexed by a surprising point of view.

Alex continued, excited that someone can talk physics with him, "The fundamental weirdness of the world is in dual nature of particles, such as photons or electrons. They behave like particles and waves at the same time. In classic double-slit experiment and Wheeler's delayed-choice experiments, one can easily see that even the act of checking the particles' state causes them to behave like a wave or like a particle at different moments in time. Isn't that weird? You can't write one single equation that will describe both: a probabilistic wave and a single particle. That is why those two theories will never be unified."

"I feel our world is unnecessarily complex. I am used to thinking that everything is for a reason. There is no reason in the existence of so many types of particles and so many 'mix-ups' such as the particle and wave duality of light, and even this speed of light relativity is not nice. It is not beautiful anymore... " said Robbie.

Alex looked at Robbie even more perplexed, as the use of the expression 'not nice' to the theory of relativity caused Alex to fall in a state of lite cognitive dissonance.

Martin came back and asked Alex if he can talk to his acquaintance. Alex and Martin quickly left. Robbie was standing alone in the middle of the deck. He decided to move from the deck area into an almost empty apartment. Robbie was an inquisitive person. He occupied a lovely and cozy sofa in the corner of the living room, took out his phone, and began searching experiments that Alex mentioned. Robbie was stunned to find out how weird the world really was, as he was browsing through the basics of fundamental particles physics.

Robbie hit an encyclopedia web page dedicated to Planck constant. "I didn't know that there is an undividable quantity of energy, mass, speed, and time! Does that mean our world is digital?" thought Robbie. He looked up the double-slit experiment's main idea. The experiment was designed to shoot photons on a receiving panel. Then scientists placed a dark screen between the photon gun and the receiving panel. The dark screen had two slits. Scientists were shooting one photon at a time, and it would create a wave pattern on the receiving panel as if photon was not a particle but a wave. Moreover, it looked like the photon was randomly choosing one slit or the other after each shooting. "Jeez, how weird is that? Bible talked about miracles. That is in the same category," thought Robbie.

Robbie noticed Scott sitting in an armchair. He was blankly watching at the large dark TV screen, holding a bottle of wine in his hand.

"Don't like parties?" Robbie asked.

Scott slowly turned to Robbie, and mumbled," Partying before the end of the world."

"Yeah, if people drink too much then the world will end," Robbie tried to make a lame joke to cheer him up.

"No, you don't understand. We are all doomed. People edit DNA as if they are Gods. Then make funny movies about zombies. It is not a joke! I bet there is a crazy guy somewhere making a killer virus right now," Scott said, trying to take a sip from the bottle.

"Oh. Don't worry. Humans always found a way to save themselves. Remember how much drama was around the nuclear weapons?" Robbie tried to cheer him up again.

"What is the sense of pushing myself, exercising, eating right, working hard, saying right things at work; You know, I am off my ADHD meds; I am sick and tired of trying to get to the next level," said Scott almost crying.

Robbie didn't know what to answer. He had his thoughts flying around the unfamiliar physics concepts he just learned. He tried to cheer up Scott once again. After a few more attempts to continue a meaningful dialog, Robbie gave up and left the room going back to the deck. Meanwhile, Scott left the place without saying goodbye to anyone.

Robbie was back home at 12pm. He was searching more about physics for a few more hours until falling asleep.

7

VERSIONS

Robbie woke up at 7:30am and arrived at work on time. He came out from the elevator and saw the HR girl surrounded by other employees; she was crying. Robbie came closer and was about to ask what happened.

"Scott killed himself," she said to Robbie before he could ask, "He made the police do it. Aimed a gun at them last night."

Robbie was frozen for a few seconds trying to process what he was just told. He couldn't fully understand how could it be that a person he had a conversation with last night is not alive anymore. Robbie suddenly realized that he must have been the last person Scott talked to. He got shivers through his spine. Robbie felt guilty for not helping Scott when he had the opportunity. He thought about Scott's parents. Robbie didn't know his parents, but he imagined that it would be devastating to lose a son like that, a diligent, responsible and kind person, whom everyone liked.

Robbie and other Scott's coworkers were invited to the funeral. It was scheduled for next Saturday. He accepted the invitation and was there on time.

Robbie saw crying relatives. He saw the black coffin, and he saw Scott. It was hard to believe he was dead. Robbie remembered his father's funeral. Pain squeezed his stomach, and shivers went through his body. He heard the familiar sobs. It was the HR girl.

"I might have been the last person to talk to him," said Robbie to the HR girl, feeling ashamed as if he was partially responsible for Scott's death.

"Oh, gosh. It must be really hard for you," said the HR girl.

A tall man in his 40s standing next to the HR girl turned to Robbie and asked quietly, "Has he said anything about depression or medicine he was taking? I am his family doctor. My name is Alan."

"Yes. Scott looked tired in the last few days. He also mentioned that he stopped taking ADHD medicine," answered Robbie.

"Oh. It is a plague of modern times. I told him that he doesn't need those. People push themselves too much, and then they ask for a drug to be able to push even further." said Alan.

The official part of the funeral was over, and guests were asked to join the luncheon. Alan got hold of Robbie to ask more about Scott's last days. They talked about Scott's signs of depression and his sudden mood changes.

"There are many theories explaining depression. From chemical in-balance to childhood trauma," said Alan.

"Is a lack of meaningful life also a cause?" asked Robbie.

Alan paused and then replied, "Yes. In a way. I have a hard time defining the purpose of life, as well," he chuckled grimly, "Still, most psychological diseases are caused by physical damage in the brain. The brain is just a body part like a heart or a liver. The brain can get sick. I worked with people whose brain was damaged in car crashes and from strokes. I could clearly see the pattern. Patients with more physical damage to the brain were expressing less human traits. The first human traits to go were speech and reasoning. There is no such thing as soul disease; you can literally see the neuron damage on MRI. It is all physical."

Robbie was astonished that with such simple words, a doctor just destroyed the concept of a soul and defined a soul as merely a complex 'brain device'.

Robbie left the luncheon early and got home by 5pm. He felt exhausted; still, he went outside with Charlie to try to calm himself down after the emotional last few days. The walk didn't help. Robbie tried watching sports. That didn't help either. The thoughts of Scott ending his perfectly ordinary and happy life were still torturing him. "Yes, he was affected by the idea that humanity will end, but it can happen in a million years from now. Maybe he couldn't find the meaning of life, and that was the actual reason? Well, I can't find the meaning of life either, but I feel alright," thought Robbie. Eventually, it was late, and he went to bed.

Robbie tried to fall asleep, but nothing helped. He took his phone and looked up 'meaning of life.' There were hundreds of versions for the meaning of life, from religious to secular, from the texts that declared that "pursuit of the meaning of life should be the only reason to live" to ones that said, "people should not seek the meaning of life."

Robbie noticed that it was not only Christianity that declared the primary purpose of life as to prepare for the next eternal life after death and to believe in only one God. Many religions had a concept of life after death and a concept of one God. "People really want to find the meaning of life if they have so many versions," thought Robbie.

After digging deeper, Robbie found out about Pragmatism, which he immediately liked. The main idea of Pragmatism was defined as 'people should only trust verifiable in real life things, and therefore, anything unverifiable had no meaning'.
According to Pragmatism, the purpose in life was stipulated by the pursuit of anything practically useful. Like many young men of his age, Robbie regarded himself as quite a cynical person. It was fashionable to be cynical these days. Robbie assumed that Pragmatism theory fitted him much better than Christianity that he leaned towards earlier.

Robbie didn't stop on Pragmatism and read more. This night's favorite version for Robbie ended up to be Hinduism's Purusartha, which declared the meaning of life as the pursuit of four: pleasure, prosperity, spirituality, and righteousness.

It was really late. Charlie was long asleep, and Robbie finally felt sleepy as well. He had a beautiful dream of Anne dressed as Parvati, dancing a happy Indian dance. She was his wife. Robbie was a rich and famous guru. He was respected for all the good he did for the poor. It was all happy and simple.

8

NO SURPRISE

Robbie woke up. It was still early morning. He decided to spend his extra time by making a more sophisticated breakfast for himself instead of usual milk and oats. He noticed his palm shaking and the knife not doing a good job cutting a tomato. "It must be because of Scott. Strange, I didn't notice that yesterday," Robbie thought.

A few days passed. After seeing death so close, Robbie felt like he needed to do something with his life, but he had no idea what that 'something' was. He was trying to analyze what must change in his tranquil existence. "I don't like my job much. I guess having a girlfriend would be nice. That should compensate for the boring job. Maybe I could build some additional source of income or have a hobby," he thought.

Robbie decided to act on the girlfriend idea as the most feasible. Robbie was about to use the most common trick in human history to get a date with a girl. He was sitting at his usual bench with Charlie at his feet. The time was precisely chosen. He was waiting for Anne to run by. Anne showed up as usual. Robbie woke up Charlie with a light kick of his foot. Old Charlie woke up grumpy as his peaceful sleep was ruined and barked.

"Hey, Anne! Charlie is happy to see you!" cried Robbie with unnatural excitement.

"He seems in a good mood," she answered, catching her breath and trying to smile.

"Anne, it might seem strange to you, but I think I like you. Do you want to have a dinner with me or something?" Robbie said very quickly, trying to make his suffering shorter while regretting the resulting awkwardly sounding question.

Anne stopped and focused on Robbie for a moment. Then she smiled and said, "Sure. Where do you want to go?"

Robbie was not planning on what should happen after revealing his feelings to her. Anne's question caught him off guard, and he was now thinking of a good place to go.

"I work at SAM. We have a new amazing exhibition of Indian art. We can meet there if you want," suggested Anne.

"Great. I've never been there. At what time?" asked Robbie; the last night's Indian dream flashed through his mind.

"We can do it Saturday around 11am," she suggested.

"OK!" said Robbie, not knowing what to say next.

"OK, see you at the entrance on Saturday then," Anne smiled and continued her jogging routine.

Saturday came fast, and Robbie met Anne at the entrance. She looked happy and cheerful as usual. She walked Robbie through the galleries with works of art from various cultures. Some looked primitive but creative, while others looked sophisticated and insightful. Anne talked with excitement about all of them.

"So you work as a guide here?" asked Robbie.

"Yes. Part-time. I am also a biology student at Seattle University. Art is my hobby, so to speak," said Anne.

"Art and biology are quite far apart," remarked Robbie.

"A bit, but also very similar. Living things are created by nature and art by people. Both are beautiful," she said with a witty smile.

They entered the section of Indian art.

"These are paintings of Amrita Sher-Gil, my favorite artist. As you can see, these are paintings that she did in Paris at the start of her career; then she moved back to India and did paintings like these on the right wall. See, how much deeper and beautiful the Indian period paintings are. She even used to say that Europe belonged to the likes of Picasso and Matisse while India belonged to her," Anne was talking with admiration.

"I actually studied art in college. I studied something I was not even excited about," said Robbie, feeling embarrassed.

Anne paused for a second and then said, "I am hungry and tired. I was the one talking all the time, ha-ha, maybe we can go eat somewhere?"

"Sure, where do you want to go?", asked Robbie.

"There is this nice artsy restaurant nearby, on 4th street. We can just walk there from here," Anne suggested.

They walked to the restaurant. Ann asked Robbie what he was doing at work. Ann asked what plans Robbie had. Robbie told her about his father and that he was doing a technical writer job, but was not entirely sure if that was the right job for him. They talked about Charlie a little as well. By the time they reached the restaurant, Robbie felt like Anne knew everything about him. Robbie suddenly realized that his whole life could be told in fifteen minutes of conversation. "Is that how much time you need to describe the life of an average person? Do I really need to be more than average?" thought Robbie.

They had a pleasant late lunch. Anne was mostly talking. She understood that Robbie had very little to say, so she tried to keep the conversation going. Anne told him that she wanted to become a molecular biologist since being a kid. Anne believed that people should not be afraid of Crispr technology, as it is still just baby steps in DNA editing.

"I had a friend at work who was scared of DNA editing and people trying to play God," said Robbie.

"Nothing can stop progress. People were terrified of nuclear weapons too. Nothing bad happened. In real life, it doesn't work like in movies. There are many secured steps someone needs to take to set off a nuke. Same with DNA, you really need to know what you are doing, and you need a billion-dollar lab to make a new virus," said Anne, timidly.

"I am still learning DNA and cell biology. Sometimes I want to grab people and force them to read a few biology books so they can appreciate the beauty of cell design. A cell is one giant factory with workers and machines", Anne passionately talked about her studies.

"It is interesting that you used the word 'design'," noticed Robbie.

"I am a minority. I am like Amrita Sher-Gil in Paris. I clearly see that DNA is a program written by something with intelligence. A programmer. There is enough evidence that evolution happened right from a single cell organism to a human. The only unsolved part is the first cell itself. Darwin lived long ago, he had no clue how complex just one single cell really was. Even the first simplest cell to be able to eat and reproduce would be insanely complex. More complex than an iPhone. So if you can say that the first cell appeared from a random mix of proteins, then you can say that the iPhone appeared from a random mix of molecules. Without intelligence, iPhone cannot appear from random molecules mixture, not in a trillion years. So it is still a mystery to me."

"I keep hearing a lot about unsolved mysteries in the natural world recently," said Robbie.

They finished their dinner and came out of the restaurant. Not knowing what to suggest, Robbie said politely, "Thank you for a great date."

"Yes. Sure. See you in the park," said Anne.

"Would you like to go out with me some other time?" asked Robbie.

"We will see. I am not sure," said Anne with an apologetic smile.

"OK. Bye, Anne," said bewildered Robbie, not knowing what else to say.

"Bye, Robbie," said Anne flatly.

They went in different directions.

9

SOLUTION

Robbie was stunned, "She treated me with compassion! That what she did!" He was angry at Anne, at himself, at the world.

He was walking in the park with Charlie. Suddenly he realized that he started the second lap of his usual route. "Now I walk in circles! Great..." said Robbie with irritation.

"Why is the world created like that? Why we need to prove something to the opposite gender? Of course... Evolution! The best will be selected to produce a better next generation. I hate this system!" he thought with anger.

"OK. Fine. Let's play this game," thought Robbie.

Robbie enumerated the ways he could achieve something 'to show off'. He didn't want to place too much effort into that 'something'. Robbie thought of what he was interested in since childhood. Robbie thought of the World of Guns game, which he enjoyed playing so much, "We play as a team. We are not great, but if we push ourselves a bit more, we can get into pro competitions. Those guys make hundreds of thousands in the pro league. Maybe I can be one of them?".

Robbie suggested the idea to the guys at the next Friday meeting. Tom was excited about the idea. Alex was for it as well while Martin was against. Martin argued that he just wanted to relax at the end of the week and nothing more. With votes three to one the team agreed to try to get to the pro league.

Tom, being a natural leader, suggested a daily practice

routine. They were to start practicing every day, both individually and as a team. It was interesting to note that Tom and Martin were leaders, though Tom preferred giving direct orders, while Martin would typically start a conversion and kind of steer people to make decisions for themselves. Alex defined himself as an individual thinker who cannot be controlled by anyone. Robbie was also leaning to Alex's position in life as he never thought of himself as a leader.

Tom said that individual training was aimed at developing specific skills of the players, while team training was intended to improve the coordination and collaboration among players. The team began exhaustive drills every second day. They were preparing for the pro competitions to be held in September. The winners would be enrolled into professional league for one year; a professional team got around 10k USD for playing in any broadcasted competitions.

The time was flying fast. All of Robbie's spare time went into the competition preparations. He continued to go to the park. He saw Anne, and they would often exchange a few words. It felt a bit awkward now, and Robbie was planning to change to a different park.

Although Martin was against the pro league, he played like a real superstar. The second best was Tom. Robbie played not bad, and Alex was kind of the weakest link. All guys complained that preparations were taking a lot of their time and energy, and it was affecting their day jobs as well.

The summer was over, and the days of qualification rounds came. The team considered itself ready. "All in! You can do it! Did you get everything? OK. Let's drink for the win!" Tom cheered up the team. The gamers drank their energy drinks and got in Tom's car. They were at the Meydenbauer Center in 30 minutes.

The guys were stunned at the number of competing teams, which came from all over the US. "So, today we should have five fights. If we win three out of five, we will go to the qualifications tomorrow. The same will happen tomorrow, and then finals will be the third day. We will fight elimination rounds on the finals day. Ten teams will get into the professional league out of about eighty participating," explained Tom.

They occupied one of the long tables arranged for the participating teams. The first round started, and the fight took around thirty minutes. They were very close to winning but lost with a narrow margin. The second round was won, and Martin was exhilarated. The only player to talk during rounds was, of course, Martin. In fact, he was the only player who was talking even between rounds, while the team was taking a break. The third round was quickly lost, and the fourth had taken a whole hour and was a narrow win. It was brutal. Martin was exhausted. "I never sweated so much in my entire life!" he exclaimed. Nobody talked about the next round. They knew it will be the decisive one. The game began and was quickly lost in seventeen minutes with a significant margin.

Completely drained and sad guys got in the car and went to downtown. Originally they planned to stay in a bar and celebrate a win, which obviously never came. Instead, Tom dropped everyone next to their places. Tom was saying about being better prepared and do more training, but everyone understood that to really get to the pro, they would need to go all-in for real, which, of course, was not an option.

Robbie got home. A soccer game was on TV.

"Professional sports are just the same rat race as any corporate job. It is just not fun," thought Robbie. He very quickly fell asleep, he was exhausted and had no dreams.

10

EVOLUTION

After Scott's death, Robbie was promoted to his position. Two new trainees, fresh out of college, were hired to be managed by Robbie. The young trainees seemed like kids to Robbie. He never had younger brothers or sisters, and he never had children. It was a completely new experience for Robbie, as he never taught anyone anything. Instead, it is he who was usually told what to do and was educated by someone more experienced. Robbie liked that new 'teacher' feeling. He enjoyed explaining the assignments to the guys and how to do them. Robbie cared about his job more, and the work seemed less boring. He worked harder and not just because there was simply more work that came with his new position.

A year passed. Robbie didn't see Anne in the park anymore. Probably she moved to some other place. Robbie's salary was raised, and he was doing even better. He had a sense of accomplishment, and an unfamiliar desire started to creep in of getting to an even higher level in the company. He entered an MBA program at a local college, which was partly sponsored by his employer.

Meanwhile, Martin did miracles with his department and was promoted to Senior Product Manager. The promotion didn't change anything in his responsibilities, but the title sounded better and, of course, it meant a higher salary bracket. He used to joke that his next title would be The Supreme Product Manager. Alex got married. The World of Guns team stopped playing the game and was dissolved. Charlie got sicker by the day and soon passed away. It was his time. Robbie felt alone as he rarely was invited to parties or events; obviously, he had no close friends and no girlfriend. He visited his mom even less as well.

A year later, when Robbie graduated from the MBA program, he invited Martin, Tom, Alex, and a few other co-workers to celebrate at his small apartment. Robbie arranged for beer and pizza, as well as some board games. It was a very humble celebration. They talked about world events, corrupt politicians, and how the country was becoming a falling Roman Empire. Everyone blamed the current president and the ruling party. That was a usual party talk among well-to-do young and educated. Robbie was more interested in the efficient theoretical principles of government rather than specific political parties or people. He fell in love with the use cases, an approach that he learned at his MBA program. In fact, Robbie discovered an entirely new world of case study analysis. He did very well in classes. At the MBA program, they would often organize classes in groups of four and give them the use cases to solve. A typical use case would describe a company that was losing money, and certain initial circumstances and details would be provided. Then a use case asked what a CEO would do to save the company. Robbie realized that he often led the group of four to solve the use case. Their team was almost always a winner. Robbie felt empowered and excited, as he felt a leader being born somewhere deep inside. Robbie described this experience to his friends at the party.

"The key to being good at case studies is to imagine in your head what is going on with the company, with all the details down to a single employee. To feel how it all works day-to-day. And try to find a simple and practical, common-sense solution," explained Robbie.

Martin asked, "Robbie, can we talk in private?"

"Sure," answered Robbie.

They came to Robbie's bedroom, as the balcony and living room were occupied.

"I am being promoted to VP. Please, don't tell anyone yet. I was thinking of you to take my place and be my Product Manager," said Martin.

"Me? Why not someone else. What about Tom. He is a true leader. What about people from other departments?" asked Robbie.

"Of course, there will be multiple people considered. Tom is definitely a no. Even though he is an outstanding programmer, no one wants to lose a great programmer to a lousy management role. Also, he is too pushy with people. I don't want to hire people from outside either; I would rather have someone I know at this position. Your MBA graduation is just perfectly timed. This will be a big step for you. I spent ten years to get to this level, and you are getting it after just two years being with the company." said Martin.

"Yes, sure. What should I do to get it?" asked Robbie. He was surprised and also excited about the opportunity.

"Well, just read a few books from my list. Get ready to answer tricky questions during the interview. Be honest; and write the best resume possible. I will recommend you specifically to the CEO. Remember that. I'll need help from the product managers like you when fighting those predators at the top," said Martin, giving a long stare.

Robbie was hired as Product Manager. Everything happened very quickly. He couldn't believe how much information he was getting right from the first day at the new position. He had to talk to dozens of people daily. He desperately tried to remember their names. When he was home, he was just chilling out on a sofa with some dumb TV shows in the background. Some days he had no energy even for that. "I am in ultimate rat race now, I like it and I am winning," suddenly realized Robbie.

A year passed. Robbie's department was doing well. Robbie developed a management style of his own. He listened very carefully to what people were saying. Analyzed every detail and gave the best possible solutions he could come up with. Robbie recorded all the memos into his phone, so he wouldn't forget any details, and followed up on everything that was happening. People called him an owl for his ability to see through.

Robbie's youth laziness disappeared. He was in his early thirties, and he was a different man now. His job was taking all of his time. He didn't have time to contemplate and think about things deeply anymore.

Once being in a coffee shop, Robbie met a buddy he studied with at the MBA program. He worked in one of the mid-sized defense companies in the Seattle area. "We are looking for a software product manager. I remember you were the software guy," he said. After learning about the opportunity, Robbie got excited as it promised a higher salary, more responsibilities, and access to the 'cool' heavy industry of planes and tanks. Robbie took a chance and got the job. It took a few months to transition. Robbie made sure when he was leaving his previous position that everything was arranged correctly and prepared for his replacement. He turned out to be a very responsible person. Everything was happening even faster now. After many years of nothing changing in his life, Robbie felt he was in the new fast-paced wonderland world of business.

He immediately dived into a new and unfamiliar defense sector universe. Another year passed, and Robbie was promoted to a director of the software department in the company. Turned out the software salespeople loved him for the ability to listen and apply their requests in the products very quickly. Robbie was friends with everyone. He had many people working for him now, and he had a sizable budget for his department to manage. He still felt as being just one tiny step in a very high ladder of the corporate world, but he also knew that it was his own step.

Robbie was sitting at his balcony of the recently purchased downtown apartment and was enjoying a morning coffee. He was taking a short break from answering emails and phone calls while looking at Seattle's beautiful skyline. Seattle was not far in the distance, it was right here. Robbie could touch it. He saw a happy young man walking down the street. Robbie sipped his coffee, and a thought flashed through his mind, "I would never be able to enjoy this coffee as much as I am enjoying it now. I am exhausted but quite happy at the same time. I am one of those who made it in Seattle. An intoxicating feeling."

11

PSALM 26:2

Weeks passed. Robbie's boss asked him to go to lunch together.

"Robbie, you know that our main customers are government people. There is something I want to discuss with you that should stay private. Will you?" asked Robbie's boss.

"Yes. Sure," answered Robbie.

They went to a local Indian restaurant and occupied a corner table. Robbie and his boss loved Indian food, and this place was famous for the best garlic Naan in Seattle. They both ordered Tandoori Chicken. The boss took out his phone, extended his hand, and looking at Robbie pressed the On/Off button until the phone turned off. Then he stared at Robbie silently. Robbie took his phone and turned it off.

"We need one person in the government to like our infantry software better than a competitor. It is an order worth 40 million. The guy manages state funds for the new infantry tactical software. He liked ours, but it looks like he is leaning toward our competitor's solution now. If the competitor gets the order, it will be game over for us in the infantry software business. Once the military is hooked up on one solution provider, it is almost impossible to change to another later. Our software is not bad, all we need is just to tweak a bit the weighs in our favor. Everybody wins," the boss was saying quickly in a quiet and intimate voice.

"So you want me to write a sales offer with a huge multiyear support discount?" asked Robbie, hoping it is just that.

"Well. I don't think it is something this guy is interested in. He simply manages government money, not his own, so a discount is not something that makes a difference for him," said the boss even quieter. Robbie saw fear in his boss's eyes.

"OK," said Robbie, not knowing what to say.

"This government guy already indicated that his relative has an LLC that manages car rentals. All you need to do is sign a contract with this LLC to provide their rental car fleet to our sales staff. A two year contract. Is this something you are willing to do for our business success? There is no risk in it," said the boss in a pleading tone.

Robbie was not sure what to reply. It was clearly a bribe that he had to give to a corrupt government official. Robbie only heard about things like that in the news. Now he was on the battlefield himself. "What was I thinking?" Robbie suddenly regretted his decision to move into defense business. "The arrangement is perfectly safe, and it is not a huge contract, either. No one will look too deep into all the connections for such a small thing," thought Robbie.

"OK," said Robbie, after a long pause. The boss smiled, clearly relieved by the reply.

"Thank you so much, Robbie," said the boss with a long stare. They quickly left the Indian place.

Robbie rambled through Seattle's streets. He thought if what he would do was actually safe. Robbie believed that it would be impossible to prove anything even if someone decided to thoroughly investigate the case. He rented the cars from a provider, and there is no connection aside from that conversation to the government software order. Robbie stopped, "If I do this, I will never be able to tell myself that I am an honest man. The act itself will stain my soul forever. Even if there is no such thing as a soul, I will not see life as bright anymore." Robbie suddenly realized that he didn't want to do it, and not because of fear but because he didn't want to morally suffer for the rest of his life.

Robbie made a definite decision to not commit the crime. He understood that most likely, he would be fired or demoted by refusing the deal, so in a way, he was sacrificing his well being for a moral reason. Robbie pondered how his finances and his mortgage would work out if he lost his job. He most certainly would have to find a new job urgently... The job would be for sure worse than what he had now. Otherwise, he had to sell the house. Robbie felt sorry for himself, remembering the pleasant feeling on the balcony a week ago. He would not be able to have that feeling again for a while. He began to flip flop on his decision and considering to do the bribe again. Then he stopped and said out loud, "Pity to oneself is the main cause of a crime."

He took the phone. He called his boss and said that he would not do that.

The next morning he came to work hoping for the miracle.

"We would like to let you go. Effective immediately. I hope you understand." said the boss.

Devastated, Robbie came home. It was still late morning. He had never been in his apartment during late mornings on a working day. The unusual sounds of a construction going on in a nearby building were heard from his window. "Strange. I didn't even know there is a construction nearby," he thought.

He called Martin asking if he can return.

"I don't think you valued my help enough... You left in just one year. No, man, sorry," Martin replied.

Robbie was sitting alone in an apartment, which he was about to lose, thinking about what he would do next.

12

I IS FOR INDIA

After trying to find a product manager job for three months, Robbie gave up on the idea. Nobody would hire him for a high-profile job after he was fired, especially since he was only two years in the well-known defense company. Robbie was sitting on a sofa in a motel room, which he rented while searching for a new opportunity anywhere in the US. Robbie was thinking. The only option was to seek a technical writer job and start his career from scratch. Robbie hated this idea as it was excruciating for him to even think of starting his career ladder climbing from the first step again. He thought of his father, who was not able to adapt to the new realities of the modern-day. Robbie was not going to make the same mistake. He was hunted into a corner and was prepared for the bold new ideas. It is incredible what people can do when nothing left to lose.

After selling the apartment, Robbie had 25k USD on hand, a leftover from the original mortgage down payment. "What can I do with this money? Not much," thought Robbie, "Maybe I could start a small shop or something like that in a cheaper country. Some island nation maybe?" A thought of being a beach kayak renter made him smile. He started to think seriously about possibilities abroad. He listed ventures he could start with that money. He thought of countries where people knew English. He thought of himself as a company with 25k in the capital and how to turn it around to be profitable again. It was his own use-case analysis. Robbie's use-case.

"VR sets are not very expensive here for an average person to buy, but probably expensive in India," a thought flashed through his brain. He had no idea why that thought came to him. Robbie started to analyze further, "India is still not expensive. They understand English there. VR sets will not be owned by most families as VR sets are relatively new. Kids will love to play those in a dedicated VR place." Robbie thought of a VR set arcade where parents with kids could come and leave their kids playing VR games for a small fee. He did a short online search on India. Turned out the top five big cities in India had those already. Robbie searched for smaller cities. He zeroed in on Pune. A smaller city in India but still huge by US standards. Pune obviously had a lot of middle-class families with kids. They did not have the VR arcade place yet.

"It is better to succeed in small than fail in big," thought Robbie.

Without any further considerations, after just two hours passed since the VR-set idea came to him, Robbie bought a one-way ticket to Mumbai. He ordered three VR sets, the best value on the market he could find. He began preparations for a big and bold move to a new country. Robbie visited an international lawyer who specialized in expats. They devised a plan for proper visa, legalization, and residency, as well as the charter for the company in India. Robbie studied how VR arcades operated in the Seattle area.

After the three long weeks, Robbie was standing outside Mumbai International Airport getting a cab, which would drive him to Pune; a few hours drive. Robbie had never been abroad.

The new images, the new language, the new sounds, and smells surrounded him from all sides. "It must be what a person would feel when setting foot on another planet," Robbie thought.

In Pune, Robbie had a meeting with a local expat who helped him get settled. Robbie connected with him just before the trip. He rented a place for the arcade next to Pune's central mall. The building had a small backdoor space where Robbie decided to live. This way, he would be able to look after the place 24/7. Robbie was extremely conservative with his money. He knew that he had to spend as little as possible for his small venture to survive the first months until business took off. Robbie hired Prasad, a local art shop owner, to help him build decorations and the large VR Arcade sign. Most of the small interior work Robbie did himself. Online instruction videos helped a lot with the essential handyman work. It was tough to focus on the final goal he had in his mind, while his thoughts were occupied by the new people and how-to-dos of living in a new country.

After just two weeks of the enormous effort, the arcade was ready. Prasad did an incredible job with the sign and other art decorations. Also, it turned out that Prasad and Robbie loved furniture making, so they did some of the furniture designs together. Robbie was excited when Prasad gave him a free bonus, which was a human-sized Ganesha statue, made of a single tree trunk piece. They installed it together at the front inner wall so everyone who was entering the place could immediately see it.

Robbie spent a lot of money on local ads. He decided to operate the arcade himself with hopes that locals will be able to understand English as he couldn't speak Hindi or Marathi. After having first visitors, whom Robbie remembered for the rest of his life, like everything first and essential, he realized the need for a local to be an operator in order to speak with the customers.

Robbie hired Prasad's son to help.

Initially, Robbie had very few visitors that didn't spend much time playing and paid pennies. He blamed himself for being a naive fool who lost everything and went to the end of the world without a good idea or plan. One day Prasad came to check on his son. He noticed gloomy Robbie, he saw almost empty arcade. He came to Robbie and said, "Your idea is interesting. People will love it. Luck is the result of patience." Robbie was grateful for the kind words. Someone's support was everything Robbie needed at that moment.

After two months, it was clear that Robbie's gamble paid off. The business was slowly gaining traction. With every new week, he noticed more people in the arcade as more people were learning about the latest entertainment center in the area.

Robbie understood that he must scale quickly to not get stuck and become 'that one local entertainment venue'. He had a few more years to scale business until VR arcades would be everywhere and then eventually would start the slow death spiral, as a new and exciting part of it waned. The competition would, for sure, drive the prices down and kill all the small venues. Robbie made plans to open more VR arcades in cities such as Surat and Nashik. He needed many more people to work for him. Robbie hoped to find someone as good as Prasad and his son.

13

BLUES

First months Robbie was so busy that he didn't have time for even a short pause to contemplate his situation. He spent five long months in Pune. Robbie's only joy was local food. He enjoyed it mostly alone. Loneliness was bothering him a lot by now. Not only he had no friends or family, but he didn't even have people he could call acquaintances. The only people Robbie talked to regularly was Prasad and his son. Prasad would often come to check how things were going and to instruct his son on how he should work better. Robbie had to defend Prasad's son from his father as he never seemed happy with his son's work.

Prasad would often complain about the difficulties of running his small art shop. He talked about politics and how great Modi was. Prasad was very proud of India's progress. He always emphasized that despite many languages that people spoke in India, the whole country was unified by Hindu religion. Robbie didn't want to remind him about the large Muslim provinces to not spoil his mood. Prasad was a very religious and proud person. He explained Robbie a lot about Hindu religion, customs, and Indian traditions.

Prasad's young son often joined the conversations, "You know, Hindu is the most computer-friendly religion. You just increment or decrement Karma with your actions. Pure math. Just like in games. Actually, some games even call their score points as Karma score."

"Never talk about Hindu like that!" Prasad yelled at his son without fully understanding what he meant.

One day Prasad invited Robbie to his house. It was a large, three-story, old house. Robbie was surprised that a small art shop owner had a house like that.

"Three families live here," said Prasad, "Mine, my brother's, and my cousin's."

"Amazing. You all get along?" asked Robbie.

"It is not a family if it doesn't have a quarrel or two," Prasad laughed.

"It is not different from people living in these modern apartment buildings where everyone gets squeezed into. People see each other and often don't even say hello in the elevator. Our three families live in one house together, but we are also the one big family at the same time," Prasad continued, emphasizing the word 'one'.

"Yeah, we are a more individualistic society in the west. Yet we have our share of fun too," answered Robbie with pride.

"Westerners are all miserable. Hindu religion has a concept of Kama. You should not take shame in taking pleasures of life, and you don't have that in the Christian world. Instead, Christians constantly blame themselves for the sins from which they can't escape. Just take your existence as it is, try to be good and embrace life's pleasures!" said Prasad.

"The physical pleasures are important, yet humans are not just about physical," said Robbie.

Prasad's wife, cousin, and their daughters served the table. All the big family came down to dinner. Robbie was having one of the tastiest dinners of his life.

Prasad's mother, the oldest member of the family, joined the party. She was barely able to walk. Prasad carefully helped her to go down the stairs. He was very tender with his mother, talking to her softly. Robbie remembered his mother, whom he left alone in Seattle. Robbie wondered if she would love to be with him in a big family like Prasad's. "Is this really good that we are so individualistic? We always think about ourselves first," thought Robbie.

Dinner was in full swing. Not everyone talked English in Prasad's family, so they often were switching and mixing between Marathi, Hindi, and English. They laughed at each other's mixed-language sentences and were sincerely happy. Robbie's head was spinning after drinking some Karnataka's wine.

"Maybe Prasad is right. We, Christians, constantly blame ourselves for our sins and therefore are unhappy by definition. We are all sinners and are doomed unless we grab Jesus's saving hand," thought Robbie. Even though Robbie identified himself as agnostic, he understood that the whole western culture was shaped and refined for centuries by Christian beliefs.

Robbie's thoughts were interrupted by a loud arguing between Prasad's wife and his cousin. They were quarreling whether Aamir Khan was more handsome than Salman Khan. Prasad yelled and interrupted them, insisting that he felt jealous even though everyone could see that he was not.

After dinner, Robbie returned to his VR place. It was very late and tranquil. Only UPS device was beeping every five seconds as its battery was running its course. Robbie bought a used UPS device to save money, turned out that it wasn't a smart move. He walked into his tiny room and dropped on the bed. He slept for three hours.

He woke up and couldn't sleep anymore. "Is that what we all really need? To be not alone? To be surrounded by family. They are so happy together!" thought Robbie with envy.

Robbie thought about reasons for such strong family bonds in India, "From birth, I was taught to think as an individual. 'I' is central in my thoughts. I even cannot think for the family. It is probably cultural and comes from my upbringing. My parents got it from their parents and so on. Maybe, it all comes from Christianity where an individual and his relation with God are at the center of all, not the family. On the other hand, I remember watching a program on religious Amish. They live in tightly-knit communities. I am sure they think in the best interest of family and community, not individual interests. Individualism is something we acquire in the mainstream culture. It is not built-in, and it is not really about religion."

Robbie looked for other examples of environments shaping people's traits, "I guess we are all the same at the beginning. All humans are the same when born. We are different because we are raised in different environments, and we become products of those environments. For example, many northern nations are famous for good architecture and engineering skills that require long term planning. Obviously because of long winters! If someone doesn't plan well in a cold climate, he will starve to death during a long winter. So those skills developed over generations. On the other hand, the Japanese are known to be perfectionists because they had so little land to care for, so maybe they optimized every foot of it. That overtime developed into perfectionism. You can trace environments shaping the traits of people everywhere..."

Robbie continued, "Individualism is definitely a product of the environment. Though pain and suffering are easier when someone is caring for you. In family, it is not a single soul but all souls connected together what matters. A network of souls so to speak." Robbie desperately wanted his soul to become part of that network. He was ready to be transformed into something else if needed. Just not to be alone. In his imagination, his soul was a lonely and dull star flying away from the constellations of other brighter and happier stars.

Robbie sobbed lying in his bed in the dark empty room. It was surprisingly quiet that night, only the UPS beeps were heard behind the wall. Robbie wanted someone to be with him, talk to him, hug him, and protect him. Someone he could call a soul mate.

14

HUMAN PROBLEM

Robbie walked along the noisy streets of Nashik. He needed to find the right place for his second arcade. Robbie considered opening the second location downtown of Nashik, just like he did in Pune, but when Robbie arrived and walked the downtown streets, he realized that it was more like a historic center and not exactly an accessible family-friendly location. Then he heard about Shubham Water World, which a lot of families visited. He took a taxi there and was very impressed with the number of people visiting the modern entertainment center. One of the nearby older buildings had a "For Rent" sign. He decided to open his arcade in that place. Preparations began. He ordered Prasad to build decorations for the second arcade. Robbie planned to move to Nashik and leave Prasad and his son to run the first location. After a month passed, when everything was ready, Robbie hired a mid-sized truck, loaded it with all the decorations and equipment and was prepared to leave Pune. Just before getting into the car, he hugged Prasad like a brother.

"Stars connected us," said Prasad. Robbie was stunned to hear that, and tears filled his eyes. "Good luck to you, Prasad. See you in a month," said Robbie.

The new location was a success. Robbie hired a local to run the place, and after just two months, Robbie was moving inland and to the north opening new locations using the same pattern. As the number of sites grew, so did the total revenue. Robbie had to visit each location monthly to resolve technical problems and do the hiring. Robbie was exhilarated. He was a true entrepreneur now. He enjoyed planning his own day and reporting to no one but to himself. Robbie felt happy despite being as lonely as before. When issues with business happened, he felt very clearly that if he didn't solve those, no one would. The responsibility was enormous.

The first problem occurred in Nashik as a torrential rain flooded the server room and destroyed all the server equipment. At another arcade location, a different issue with corrupt fire inspectors demanding a bribe bothered Robbie. The worst-case happened in Surat location. Robbie noticed that the place was full of kids playing, every time he visited the site, but monthly revenue was meager. He stayed in the hotel across the street from the arcade and counted the visitors. He was surprised to find out that only half of the visitors contributed to the revenue. The operator was stealing. He had to fire the guy. Robbie was unable to keep up with the mounting numbers of problems as the business grew. He needed a right-hand man or better a dozen of right hands.

He came to Pune to see Prasad. They were having dinner at his house.

"I need somebody I can trust to solve issues at various locations. Can I trust you?", asked Robbie.

"Yes, Robbie, I always served you honestly. And if something is wrong, you always know where to find me," Prasad answered with gratitude.

"I am thinking to change the charter so you can get 5% of the income. I am also ready to give you a power of attorney to help solve various issues on sites. I cannot do everything alone. I haven't been home for a year. I want to visit home from time to time. It would be great to have at least a week to breathe. This offer is earned by your service, but also it means you will have a huge responsibility to run it all well," said Robbie.

"Yes. I already know all the aspects. I guess I need to talk to my wife as I will be traveling a lot," answered Prasad. They shook hands. Then Prasad hugged Robbie.

A year passed, business growth slowed, and it happened faster than Robbie predicted. VR was not as new anymore. Also, VR was becoming affordable for the middle class to own.

Prasad was not as good a manager as Robbie hoped. Some locations stopped bringing profit at all. Numerous issues with many sites hurt business a lot. Even though Robbie had more free time, he still didn't travel to the US. He could only name a few days a month without some new emergency occurring somewhere.

Despite his constant business worries, Robbie tried to find some time to help the poor. As he expanded his operations inland, he saw more and more people that worked hard but still stayed extremely poor. Robbie talked to them in his basic Hindi. He gave their kids books so they could be literate and could find a better job. This was a different kind of poor compared to the primarily drug and laziness induced poor of the US.

Prasad was traveling inland, and Robbie decided to do a

check on Surat location, which was bringing very poor profits again. He did the same trick as before and stayed in the hotel across the street. Robbie was counting the customers. Suddenly he saw Prasad entering the place. Robbie ran down the stairs, crossed the road, and looked inside the arcade. Prasad was getting cash from the operator, so Robbie opened the door and rushed into the room confronting Prasad.

"What are you doing, Prasad?" screamed Robbie. Prasad turned to Robbie with fear in his eyes. Then he lowered his head and began crying.

"Can we talk in private?" asked Robbie. Prasad and Robbie came up to Robbie's hotel room.

"How long have you been stealing?" asked Robbie.

"I couldn't resist that. It is just too much money to resist! I swear I was an honest man my whole life," wept Prasad.

"We will have to part our ways. You will have to return 5%, and I will not report this to the police," said Robbie.

"You are a very kind man, Robbie. Thank you," cried Prasad.

"You are a good art maker. Live in peace and do your art," said Robbie.

Robbie got his 5% back from Prasad. He never met him again. Robbie thought about Prasad almost every day. How an honest and loving parent, a craftsman with pure soul got corrupted by money. He remembered his boss in the defense company. The boss was a hard worker, he earned his Ph.D. early, then he worked diligently through the years to get his position, he was a family man with three kids, he had everything in life, and yet he got corrupted too. Even his friend Martin was weaving a mafia-like web of useful people to become the boss of the company one day. "Are all humans inherently bad and sinful?" thought Robbie with despair, "Or maybe it is just people's naivety that allows for people to deceive and betray? What if there were no naive people at all and everyone would suspect everyone else? Then there would be no liars and manipulative people at all. It would be impossible to lie or betray. Is being naive a sin?"

15

MONOLITH 1

After almost two years in India Robbie was homesick. He didn't want to go anywhere but home. He even didn't want to move to California anymore, where he could ride a bike at any time of the year, enjoying sunny weather. He only wished to be in one place only - Seattle. He missed his mom and was hoping to find Anne and to show her what he managed to achieve in the past years. Robbie wondered why he cared about Anne. He barely knew her. Robbie heard stories about people meeting each other for the first time and feeling like they knew each other for the whole life. Robbie felt the same for Anne. He couldn't explain it. He even thought that all the hard work he was doing for the last years and his push to become successful was only to impress her. "That would look so strange to a computer brain. Why would that silly human work like crazy for so many years to just impress one girl he barely knew," chuckled Robbie.

Robbie thought a lot about successful people and how they made it in their home towns, "I didn't think just how important home really was. Truly you need to lose something before you fully understand the value of what you lost. Gates and Buffet were very successful in their hometowns. Why would someone need to leave his home? Home is the source of endless energy and inspiration. I surely can find something to do in Seattle. No matter how good India is, it is not my home. I need to come back!"

Robbie was exhausted by running a crumbling business alone. He decided to sell it while it was worth something. Robbie hired an international consultancy company in Mumbai, which would find the buyer for his chain of VR arcades. The estimated price was 350k USD. It was not bad for a young man in his mid-thirties.

Robbie already had a plan of what to do with the money in Seattle. He was hoping to start an artisan furniture shop. He learned a lot about woodworking from Prasad. Of course, Robbie remembered various techniques for wood handling that he learned from his father. He was preparing designs and sketches, excited about the new chapter in his life. "Life is amazing because you can do anything you want," Robbie praised Martin's optimism.

Robbie remembered himself being a young, cynical, and clueless child, who just entered the adult world seven years ago. By now, Robbie tried the corporate life and entrepreneurship. He saw foreign lands and different kinds of people. Robbie had confidence in his abilities. He knew that with enough effort, he could achieve a lot. In fact, he could do anything. "I couldn't have imagined how complex and colorful everything truly is. I thought I knew life back then. How foolish I was," thought Robbie now.

Robbie was visiting the consultancy office in Mumbai in order to meet with the potential buyer for his company. Robbie was the sole owner of the limited liability company that was running all the arcades. Being a foreigner, he had a pretty complex legal setup to be able to own and run the company in India all by himself. The laws of India required at least two people to form a company, one had to be an Indian resident. The solution for such situations was often offered by consultancy companies that provided nominal directors. It was all legal but sufficiently complex to be able to set it up without a lawyer. Robbie remembered the sophisticated bribery schema for the defense company that used an LLC to channel the money. It is amazing how creative the lawyers are. "Governments create laws, and there are always plenty of lawyers that find ways to work around those. A very creative job," thought Robbie.

Robbie used the consultancy company for his company's taxes as well. He still wanted to know what was going on financially, so he had to read a book about accounting just to have an idea of his finances. In the opening chapter, the book told the story of the double-entry bookkeeping system birth in the Jewish community during the middle ages. Robbie was fascinated by how ingenious yet simple the idea was to keep two sides of the ledger in balance: left side for assets and right side for liabilities and equity. Holding the sides in balance not only allowed the self-check for mistakes but provided a clear understanding of a business's health. Robbie was getting an idea that anything humans created was beautiful and exciting, provided you learned enough about the subject.

Robbie came to the consultancy early. A secretary served him coffee and asked to wait for twenty minutes. Robbie went through some magazines on the table. He opened the Science magazine where an article about quantum entanglement was describing how two entangled photons interacted across immense distances without any time delay. Robbie got immediately interested as memories about his physics investigation rushed back. The article described a recent experiment where scientists were flipping the state of one entangled photon while recording the state of another entangled photon at a great distance. The other photon instantly flipped its state without any time delay at all when the first photon was 'touched'. The two photons 'interacted' faster than the speed of light. "This world just doesn't make any sense. Quantum physics is crazy," thought Robbie, remembering the double-slit experiment. After reading the article, he tossed the magazine back on the table.

Robbie glanced at his phone to check the time and continued his reasoning, "Why the speed of light even exists? Why motion is limited by some fixed speed? Why PI constant is exactly that specific number and why Planck constant is that specific number? There are many 'Whys' and very few answers. People are inherently curious, inquisitive creatures. They can find mysteries, beauty, and patterns in everything..." Robbie discovered the ability to see the inner beauty in all human inventions beginning with art and physics and all the way to seemingly 'boring' accounting and law.

A bold athletic middle-aged man of average height came into the office. His face and body were lightly tanned. He was wearing a blue t-shirt, classic gray shorts, and black canvas sneakers.

"Ah. Good day, Mr. C. ", the secretary greeted the man. Then she turned to Robbie and said, "Robbie, this is your buyer, Mr. C. He kindly asked to stay anonymous. I hope it is not a problem."

16

MR. C.

"Robbie, I'm happy to see you. I heard a lot about you. Do you think it is a good time to have lunch together and discuss the deal?" asked Mr. C. in Californian accent mixed with some other accents Robbie couldn't identify.

"I don't know any good restaurants here in Mumbai. I rarely visit this city," answered Robbie studying the buyer.

"I know some good ones. You are, I assume, OK with Indian food?" said Mr. C. with a welcoming smile.

"Of course. I love it!" said Robbie.

They got into a taxi and arrived at one of the highest buildings in Mumbai. The restaurant was on the top floor. It was a small cozy place. Mr. C. suggested to try their specials, Robbie agreed, and Mr. C. made the order.

"Your business is suffering from both the fundamental decline of demand and scaling issues. I have ideas on how to solve both by merging your centers into other entertainment ventures I own here. That is why this deal is a win-win for both of us. I am happy to pay 300k for everything," Mr. C. immediately talked about the deal with a serious and fixated look.

Robbie took a moment to think about the offer and suggested 330.

"Robbie, no one will offer pretty much any money for the

dying business like yours. It is like buying Blockbuster stores when video streaming was coming. You have no options, while I have many other options. I can buy some other entertainment franchises to expand, so my last offer is 300k. I already did all the calculations. It is truly my last and only offer," said Mr. C., with all seriousness.

"OK... I agree to sell for 300k," Robbie said with a reluctant and hesitating voice. In fact, Robbie had no clue how much his business was really worth. He had a wide range of numbers in his mind.

"Great. Now we can relax and have a pleasant lunch," Mr. C. said cheerfully.

The food was served. Robbie thought of a topic to discuss.

"I am from Seattle. I noticed that you have a Californian accent. I once dreamed of moving to California. I was tired of gloomy Seattle weather. Though, I dream of returning to Seattle now. Don't need any other place, not in this world... " said Robbie trying the tastiest Dosa he ever had.

"I was raised by Californian parents, but most of my life I spent abroad. I come from a business family. We traveled a lot. Running a business requires a lot of moving around as you probably noticed yourself," Mr. C. smiled.

"It was very challenging for me to keep all locations working smoothly. Is that just in India so difficult?" asked Robbie feeling that Mr. C. had much more experience in business.

"No, no, India has nothing to do with it. Business is hard. It is in the same category as Darwin's survival of the fittest. We all fight for survival. This world is designed like that. The trees compete with other trees, trying to grow higher than their neighbors and get more sunlight. It is funny that we, humans, enjoy the calm walks in parks. Nature relaxes us. While in reality, it is one endless fight for survival! It is a kill zone all around us. Trees compete to grow taller and take better spot under the sun killing weaker ones. They fight for a better water source with their roots underground too. They use every last drop of that water just to get a bit higher than their neighbors. Endless fight for survival indeed. A brutal, brutal design. So do us. The people. The greatest fools are the new generations obsessed with the concept of the 'safe place'. They continuously seek that safe place on Earth. Ha, ha, ha. There is no safe place. They think sticking with a stable day job, and living humbly will protect them against the elements." talked Mr. C. sipping the wine and studying Robbie all at the same time, "Companies also compete, and there is no time for complacency with them either. It is particularly hard in business because you already have the tall trees around, they are those big corporations. Your little startup is just a tiny little bush growing under a huge canopy of oak trees. It is especially hard to start a business in this gig economy now. You have monopolies everywhere. Lobbyists, funded by big business, push for complex regulations that make the minimal legal burden impossible for small companies. They even push for a shorter work week and higher minimum wage these days. That will work out just fine for big business but imagine a small startup where people legally required to work very few hours. Another barrier for entry. You see? " explained Mr. C., changing his attention from Robbie to the beautiful ceiling of the restaurant. His inquisitive expression quickly changed to a happy and tranquil one.

"That is quite a world view. It sounds like the world is unfair. What is fair then? What would be the fairest way to organize the society?" asked Robbie.

"Well. All people could just agree one day to not compete at all. And if someone tries to compete to be shot immediately. Ha, ha. If no one competes with anyone else, then we would finally be able to relax and do stuff for fun. I don't know if you will be able to find a good doctor, though in such a world," said Mr. C.

"But seriously. What do you think is the best way to rule the world?" persisted Robbie.

"Ah. The ultimate challenge of how to rule," said Mr. C. with a candid look and asked, "Do you think, Robbie, humans are fundamentally good or evil?" Mr. C. continued without waiting for Robbie's reply, "People invented many ways to rule. The current world standard is democracy. It is kind of fair. Well, at least it is fair for the majority. The minority will always suffer in democracy. Don't forget that democracy is very slow, as well. If you have a democratic country fighting a fast, modern war with a dictatorship and provided both countries are equally powerful and not corrupt, then democracy will lose the war just because of the slow decision-making process. The majority in the democracy will be unwilling to take the necessary pains of the war, while a dictator just shoots anyone who is not willing to fight. Ah, and democracy can easily be controlled by elites via manipulations of public opinion through media and such. I am sorry, you just started my favorite topic for restaurant discussions," Mr. C. laughed and took a sip of wine. He was clearly in a good mood.

"Then dictatorships in all forms, including all those kings, tzars and supreme leaders are very efficient, as long as, the leader at the top is 'good', but once he dies or removed by some other means then the whole country goes into the garbage bin, because the top-down controlled hierarchy that they built becomes headless, like a chicken that is running on a backyard after its head was chopped off. Moreover, a good person can come to power, but time passes, and he gets corrupted by all that wealth and unrestricted full control, and we suddenly have a 'bad' guy with the unlimited power at his hands. Dictators usually control through fear..." Mr. C. stopped talking and poured himself a second glass of wine and lit a cigarette.

"I love India. They still allow smoking in restaurants," said Mr. C. He was visibly enjoying his lunch a lot. Robbie wondered how Mr. C. spent his night dinners if he had so much fun during a business lunch.

Mr. C. continued, "India is a wonderful country. They still value family and community a lot. If you look at history, the community mattered so much to all nations. This so-called civilization destroyed the importance of the community. Only some in the US still preserves that. Amish, for example. No one needs to take a thirty-year mortgage in Amish. They gather together, the whole village comes, and they build a new house for a newly married couple. They build it in under a month for a few thousand dollars, while the so-called civilized world lost the value of the community completely and depends on the state. Moreover, the civilized modern world is losing the value of family too. Singles numbers are growing while the family is not considered a sacred thing anymore. I guess, it is quite good for people like me. When each individual is on their own, then he or she becomes more vulnerable and easier to control. They make better workers and consumers too. Anyway what was your question again?" asked Mr. C. lighting another cigarette.

"So what is the right way to rule?" persisted Robbie as he was getting even more curious.

"The right way, if it were possible, would be God's ruling. God is like a dictator, only guaranteed to be always good and alive," said Mr. C. smiling, and continued, "Since God doesn't exist, the human race is suffering. We try to invent new imperfect ways to rule. Capitalism is flawed since it eventually ends up in just a handful of corrupt monopolies that destroy the true competition. Communism ends up being a corrupt totalitarian structure which doesn't benefit hard working. Nothing works! I would say the most efficient human way to rule so far is through nobility. What it means is that you form a class of people in the country. The upper class. They know each other through family relations and long-running family history. They learn from childhood how to be noble, to be honest, and responsible for their actions; otherwise, their family history will be tainted forever. They learn patriotism and love for their country. They become incorruptible right from their childhood. If you read books from seventeenth to nineteenth centuries, nobility was a big deal back then, and a reputation was defended on duels. Noble people are, in a way more valuable than religious. Both will not steal. Religious will not steal because they are afraid of all-seeing God with whom they have a personal relationship; nobles will not steal just because they are nobles. Unfortunately, the human population keeps growing, the value of one individual is falling; we live in faster times, and this nobility thing is not so much in fashion anymore. We live in dangerous times. We live in times of crazy 'democratic dictatorship', and people have to be in line with what you are supposed to do and how you are supposed to behave in majorities' opinion, and how many likes you get. The truth is independent of how many people upvoted you ."

"The United States was very successful historically, and it is a true democracy. There are special laws to break big companies apart, which helps to fight the flaws of capitalism. If that fails, there is always some extreme measure that democracy can vote for, such as Death Tax. If a rich person dies, the majority of wealth can go to the state or some fund, instead of going to descendants. This way, monopolies cannot really get formed over time," suggested Robbie.

"Ah, youth. You're such an idealist. When someone is young, he is full of energy, plans, hopes, and ideas. Well. Actually, I know some young people that are old already and some old people that are still young and enthusiastic. I guess it is just a question of being a creative one," said Mr. C. pausing and trying to collect his thoughts. He continued, "United States Constitution was written by noble elites. The current two-party system serves as a filter to ensure no random people from the street can get to power. So I think noble elites are in control. I do hope we still have the 'noble' part of 'noble elites'. Don't forget that Rome fell because of nobility disintegrating. Very soon, corruption and barbarity ensued after they lost that essential 'noble' part," said Mr. C. lighting his third cigarette.

"Nobility is not fair. You shouldn't just get nobility through a title inherited from your parents. Nobility should be earned by the actions of a person. Like knighthood was given by queen for good deeds or something similar. Regarding the two-party system, that is not set in stone. US constitution doesn't require just two parties. We have the crowdsourced funding for the elected politicians now. The country is alive, the country is changing," suggested Robbie with optimism.

"I think it would really be nice to let AI rule us all," suggested Mr. C. being visibly tipsy by now.

"We could program AI to be honest and not take bribes and to be noble. Essentially just rule everything like God," Mr. C. paused, thought about something and continued, "No need for elections, voting and all that other nonsense. Oh, and regarding your original question on how to scale your business. Just surround yourself with noble souls if you can find any, and delegate to them as much as you can."

Mr. C. was about to light another cigarette, but he stopped when he almost pulled it out of the pack. Looked at it with the saddest stare, like it was his last hope that he was about to lose. Mr. C. put the cigarette back with one quick move. Then he looked at Robbie and said with sadness in his voice, "You know what, Robbie. Everything doesn't matter much. We live in a world where no one ever will be happy no matter what he does. Don't you see that? We're always full of desires we can't fulfill and fears we can't hide from."

They were done with lunch and took a taxi back to the consultancy to sign papers. After the official signing was over, they shook hands, and Robbie was about to leave. Mr. C. asked Robbie with his soft, kind voice, "I'm curious, what was the single most complex thing you ever did, Robbie?"

Robbie thought for a moment and said, "It is, of course, the arcades business, but I will create something else soon. I know."

17

SEATTLE

After the flight from Mumbai to Tokyo, Robbie searched for his plane to Seattle. Seeing his Seattle bound plane already at the gate waiting for him to board, Robbie got shivers in his body. Entering the plane, Robbie felt that he was already back home as the plane was full of Americans talking with New York, Texas, and California accents. The nine-hour flight seemed short to Robbie even though he didn't manage to sleep.

Robbie got tears in his eyes when he felt Seattle's refreshing spring raindrops on his face. He never thought he would miss that rain so much.

Robbie visited his mom. She still worked in the warehouse and lived in the same rental. They had occasional calls when Robbie was in India, but being together was a totally different experience.

Robbie bought a small condo for himself and decided to buy one for his mom. He was sorry for her as now he clearly saw how hard it was for mom these days and also in the past when Robbie was just a careless kid. Back then, mom worked hard just to let him go through college. She lost all her savings, helping her son to take the first steps into the adult life. These days, she still worked hard at the age when people should not. Mom accepted the gift; she not only was grateful but also proud of her son.

Robbie rented an old warehouse for his woodworking. A month passed, and his first set of hand-crafted tables and chairs was ready. Initially, he didn't feel comfortable living in Seattle despite being so eager to come back. He was too worried if his furniture idea was right and it would allow him to live off it. People loved his furniture and were buying in sufficient quantities to enable him to do that full time. He didn't need to worry after all.

It was a joy waking up in the morning and plan his day deciding what to make and at what time. He did frequent breaks appreciating his coffee on the balcony. Robbie created the new sketches and made unique pieces of furniture by trial and error. He loved his new job, which allowed him to live humbly yet enjoy every single day. "What if my father started this after he was fired? What a different life it would be for him," thought Robbie.

Robbie often felt overwhelmed with memories of his time in India. He always had India at his heart. Almost all of his furniture had Indian motives. One day the thought came to him of creating a huge dining table with the glass top and wood-carved map of India underneath. The map would have all the significant India's landmarks and each city he visited. He carved Savitribai Phule building for Pune, Temple Sikhara for Nashik,

Swaminarayan Temple for Surat. Of course, he didn't omit the magnificent Taj Mahal for Agra. It was a massive project that he was doing in his free time or when taking breaks from the customer orders.

Robbie felt accomplished, strong, and confident in his future. He wanted to find Anne. She was another reason for his return to Seattle. He couldn't get her out of his heart even though his mind was saying that it was ridiculous to contact her out of the blue after so many years. First, Robbie checked the art gallery where she used to work. No one managed to help him, and the HR person got suspicious and asked him to leave.

Robbie searched online for 'Anne, University of Washington, biology, alumni' and started to go through the former students. He narrowed down the list to five Annes matching the graduation years he had in mind. When Robbie gathered the last names for all the Annes, he opened the LikedIn professionals network web site and searched there. He found his Anne. She worked as a lab technician in an NGO called New Age DNA Research Center.

Robbie entered a small two-story research building and asked a lady at the front desk if he could see his Anne. The lady took the phone and began dialing; suddenly, Robbie got second thoughts about the whole idea. He realized that it would look very strange if Anne saw him here. Without saying anything, Robbie ran out of the building. He decided to wait in his car until Anne had lunch, then he would meet her outside.

At around 1pm, he saw Anne coming out of the building. She was reading something on her phone while seeing nothing around. She wore a standard office outfit, a white blouse, and light blue pants. Anne didn't change. She looked exactly the same as he remembered her, yet something was different. The only 'logical' difference Robbie noticed was the way she walked, timidly and slow. He didn't see her usual cheerful, vigorous moves. She was almost floating along the street, making smooth and cautious steps. Robbie decided to pretend that he met her accidentally. He left the car, crossed the road, and ran behind the corner, which Anne was about to reach. When she reached the crossroad, Robbie rushed towards her.

"Hi, Anne!" said Robbie.

Anne lifted her head and looked at Robbie, immediately recognizing him. She smiled and asked, surprised, "Robbie, Hi! How are you? I haven't seen you in years!"

"Yeah. I missed you in the park. You live in this neighborhood now?" Robbie asked, trying to stay unemotional and pretend he knew nothing about her.

"No, I work here. Out for lunch. Going to grab some sandwiches," Anne answered, smiling.

"I don't live here either just was meeting a friend," Robbie lied.

"Were you a gentleman who asked for me at the front desk?" Anne asked.

Robbie already had his heart pounding, and now he felt completely frozen.

"Yes. Sorry," Robbie apologized not sure if an apology was appropriate.

Anne stared at him for a few seconds and said, "Do you want to have lunch together? They make great sandwiches here."

Robbie happily agreed, and they went together. Robbie told

Anne about his meteoric rise in his first company, and then about the job change and his tragic lay off at the defense company. He told her a lot about his India adventure and his new woodworking plans. She was listening quietly. They reached the restaurant, and she ordered sandwiches for both. They sat on a bench in the park across the road. The mid-day sun was warm and pleasant.

"My biology career didn't work out like I planned. I stuck as a lab technician," said Anne biting sandwich hard and melancholically looking at kids playing on the playground.

"I was too optimistic and naïve back then. I thought I would graduate, write an amazing paper, get hired in one of those DNA startups, or become a professor at MIT. The world would be mine," she smiled sadly.

"Well, you still work in your field," said Robbie.

"Lab technicians are not doing real science. Most of the day, we just wash Petri dishes and do the same repetitive measurements," said Anne.

"You know. You are not the first scientist who sounds so pessimistic. We had Alex at my first job, and he gave up on physics," said Robbie.

"We all know the great scientists of the past; they were my inspiration when I was little. It was easier in a way back then for them. There were so many things still to discover, and many of those things could be discovered by just one person with a garage lab. Now you need these large teams and million dollar budgets to do experiments. The science is institutionalized, slow, and not as creative. I think they declined my grant not because I am a girl, of course, but I think they might have despised me because I had these ideas of DNA created by someone intelligent," Anne was jabbering as if trying to confirm her belief in some 'other' reasons for her failure.

"Anne, forgive me for being straight with you, but there are still plenty of mysteries to uncover, and I believe some of those mysteries can be solved just by the power of one's mind. Trust me, if someone came up with a groundbreaking idea or invention, no one would care about an inventor's age, skin color, or whether the discovery was made by a man or a woman. I was in business, and businesses are often being attacked by feminists and other groups. I honestly don't know a business owner who wouldn't be happy to hire a brilliant scientist male or female, black or white, as long as he or she would contribute to the bottom line," said Robbie looking at Anne and trying to understand why she looked different to him now. Then he realized that Anne didn't change. It was Robbie himself who changed over the years.

"Yeah, maybe you are right. Feminists, for sure, go too far sometimes, maybe they even hide entitlement in their cause. I'm not a naive girl anymore. I understand how the world works now. I find myself very cynical these days," said Anne with sadness.

"I am actually the opposite. I was a very cynical and apathetic person when I was in my twenties. Now I love life, and I call myself a romantic optimist," blurted Robbie suddenly realizing that fact about himself.

"Oh. It is time to go back to work," said Ann, taking a glance at her phone.

As they walked back to Anne's work, they talked about everything that happened to them during all those years since their first date. Anne was not as talkative now, and Robbie talked most of the time. Seattle was busy as Tuesday's midday was in progress. Millions of people were doing what they were supposed to do, or at least what they thought they were supposed to do. Hundreds of thousands of people were having conversations and exchanging information, synchronizing their knowledge about things, making their brains similar. Some people had fun.

"Do you want to have dinner together sometimes?" Anne asked when they reached her work.

"Yes," said Robbie.

"Tomorrow, 7pm?", asked Anne.

"Yes," said Robbie.

18

WHAT IS STRONGER?

They married when the first warm and sunny days of April came. It was a small ceremony with only the closest family and friends. After the ceremony, Robbie and Anne left to Mexico and spent their happiest ten days of honeymoon there. Robbie's son, Aron, was born next year. As for any man who becomes a father, it was a significant change. He felt responsible for the well-being of another little human now. In fact, two human beings, as Anne quit her job and was looking after baby, she also maintained the house and helped Robbie with his business.

Robbie and Anne lived happily and quietly. The second baby was in plans. They mostly kept to themselves, sometimes visiting their parents and old friends, or going out into the city. It was July, and it was time for the Seafair Torchlight Parade festival in Seattle. They decided to come downtown and check it out.

They drove to Seattle's center, parked their car, which was not an easy task. The city was full of other parade-goers. They walked the downtown streets; Robbie had their boy in toddler carrier. The parade was already in progress, and it was hard to see anything behind the standing crowds of people. They walked along the street, trying to find the right spot. Robbie saw a young couple with a baby of Aron's age. The man had his boy in the toddler carrier just like Robbie's. The man looked familiar; it was Tom.

"Tom. Hi! Anne, this is Tom, I worked with him at my first job," said Robbie.

Tom and his wife turned and Tom, immediately recognizing Robbie, exclaimed, "Tanks forever, buddy! Look, you also got a boy!"

"Are you still at the same place?" asked Robbie.

"No, man. I left a year ago, we are making a blockchain startup now. It helps with online stock market transactions," explained Tom.

"Oh, wow! How are the other guys doing? Alex, Martin?" asked Robbie.

"Haven't you heard? Martin was appointed CEO of the company two years ago. Then the board fired him a year later for poor financial results. It turns out when you are running a company, the intrigues and right connections are not as helpful to make a profit," said Tom. He put his kid closer to little Aron so they could interact a bit. It was cute how Robbie's boy became immediately excited, his eyes opened wide, and he touched the other boy's nose and cheek.

"As for Alex. He got fired when the company struggled to

make profits a year ago. His wife left him long before that. He sits home now, plays games, and smokes weed. I think he just didn't have that will to fight through hard times. Remember, even in the game, he was not a real fighter. Listen, maybe we can have dinner sometime, all six of us?" asked Tom.

"Come to our place!", suggested Anne.

Two young salt-of-the-earth families decided to meet next Saturday.

Tom and his wife arrived at Robbie&Anne's place as was agreed. Robbie and Anne were happy to have guests. They didn't have many visitors. Robbie showed all the beautiful wood crafts that he was working on. Tom was very impressed with the unfinished India map table, which Robbie was already making for two years.

Anne and Tom's wife went outside to watch kids play and chat together as girls usually like to do. Tom and Robbie stayed inside drinking beer and having a conversation about blockchain and financial markets.

"I would've never guessed that you would be doing financial software, Tom," said Robbie.

"I always loved making games. Interestingly, making AI for games is very similar to making modern financial robo-adviser software. Both use AIs to analyze tons of data and make decisions. It is all mathematically based on game theory and probabilities. We also use blockchain to perform actual purchases and sales of stocks as a sort of digital ledger," said Tom.

"Do you like your new job?" asked Robbie.

"I like it, but I also feel it is a bit senseless," answered Tom.

"Senseless?" Robbie was surprised.

"Yes. I realized, after writing tons of code, that math is not enough. I use a lot of math like statistical analyses and probabilistic decision trees, but they are weak against a concept of 'standing your ground'. Game theory, decision trees, and all the algorithms that help producing the 'right' decisions are nothing compared to a firm belief. Just that conviction is enough to win. For example, you are a completely rational decision-maker of one country, and you are logically deciding whether to attack another country. If the decision-maker of that other country is assumed to be completely rational and smart just like you, then you can do calculations and decide whether to attack or not, purely based on probabilities and the estimate of each other's strength. Now if the ruler of that other country is a mad man, or if you know that he has a firm belief in its own righteousness, then the game theory is helpless in making the right decision cause you know that he will go to the end regardless. Moreover, if both of those rulers are crazy, and they begin fighting each other. No math can work out the outcomes. Did you notice that the 'strong belief' is somehow very similar to a 'madman' from the mathematical point of view?" said Tom sarcastically.

"I guess the same logic applies to stock trading?" assumed Robbie.

"Absolutely," confirmed Tom, "I also tried neural networks. Those worked way better! When I built a neural network and taught it to react to the input parameters based on many years of accumulated financial data, then I got incredible results! The funny part is that I have no idea why that AI works so well. I have no control over it! AI is incredible. You build the infrastructure, feed tons of data to it and then it goes on its own.

It is kind of scary too cause I am the creator of AI, but I have no clue about how it works."

"It could be an interesting startup idea to develop a good visualizer for the thought process in AI," suggested Robbie.

"Yes. Sure. This field evolves very quickly. We might even see AIs developing new AIs. I heard recently that they developed microchips to emulate huge blocks of neurons, so the brain simulation goes way faster on that new hardware. The brain is nothing more than a device that takes disorganized data and draws conclusions," continued Tom.

Anne, Tom's wife, and the kids came back from the backyard, happy and loud.

It was time for the guests to go. When Tom's family left Anne hugged Robbie and told him, "What a nice couple and the kids played so well. We need to see each other more often. Tom's wife was so impressed with your table. It is a true work of art. I can't wait to see it completed."

"I will finish it. They are one happy family. Aren't they? Pleasant people. We can definitely meet regularly," agreed Robbie.

Anne continued, "Tom's wife said that she loves him more with every passing year, and initially when she met him, she didn't even pay attention to him."

"I guess some people are like hidden gems. You love them more as you know them better. I can see Tom is an interesting person. Tom was always driven by some projects of his own. Never sitting still. Just like Martin. Only Martin was more about communicating and manipulating people, while Tom was more about making stuff work. He is also one I could definitely trust.

A reliable person and always full of ideas," said Robbie helping Anne with dishes. Robbie and Anne were cleaning up after the guests together. They talked more about their visitors and were planning tomorrow's day. Later that evening, they watched their favorite TV show, and both fell happily asleep before the end of the episode.

19

...AND THE WHOLE WORLD LIES IN THE EVIL ONE

The next day, Anne was driving on highway 90 to a doctor's appointment for Aron's regular check. There was a high-speed crash with another car, which changed the lane unexpectedly as its driver had a heart attack. Anne was alive after the impact and died in the horrible fire, desperately crying for help. They found her protecting her son, covering him with her body. It was the only reason why their child survived. Nonetheless, Aron was severely burned. He was saved after many surgeries performed by dedicated and talented doctors. Unfortunately, he would never be able to see, hear, or speak. The fire severely damaged both of his lungs, eyes, and the following infection destroyed his hearing. Doctors called his survival a miracle.

After Anne's funeral ceremony was over, and everyone left, Robbie stayed alone in the house. Aron was still in the hospital. Robbie was crying and rambling around the empty rooms. He tried very hard to stay 'decent' among guests during the ceremony, and now, when left alone, he completely lost control over himself. Robbie couldn't stand staying in the house, so he left the house and wandered through the neighborhood.

The next day nothing changed. Robbie tried alcohol. He was falling asleep for a few hours, and then he would wake up facing the heartbreaking reality. A few more days passed. He poorly remembered what was going on in the previous days. He was trying to understand, like so many before him, why the world was so cruel and unforgiving.

Aron was released from the hospital after two months of surgeries and burns treatment. He was staying with grandma. Robbie couldn't watch his son; it caused him unbearable pain. It was enough seeing him the first time with the horrible burns across his face and body. Robbie stayed alone in his house most of the time now. His mind was drifting.

Robbie stopped working on his orders. The only thing that was letting him continue to live was the table. He worked on it all the time when he was awake. It was the only way to stop the hell in his head. As he worked, his whole life passed through his mind as he replayed it over and over again.

"What kind of sadistic God would allow for all this to happen?" thought Robbie with anger, "What is the reason to live if we all die anyway sooner or later?"

As time was passing, Robbie got angrier at God even more. He remembered the homeless person he saw in the park. Robbie looked around the empty house and spoke aloud with resentment to God, "Why that drug addict, a mad man with no soul, was allowed to live while you brutally murdered my wife and scared an innocent child?" Then Robbie cried, "There is no God. It is all just a random chance. That is the only explanation!"

A few months passed. Robbie visited his son at grandma's house. Nothing changed. Doctors confirmed that the thermal damage to Aron's eyes and ear canal was permanent and he would be deaf-blind for the rest of his life. Robbie wanted to escape the pain, but he didn't know how to achieve that. When Anne and Aron were with him, he didn't fully comprehend how important they were to him. Now, without them, he felt a physical need to have them both back, to have everything like it used to be. Somehow Aron, in his current state, was not what Robbie needed. Robbie felt ashamed to think of Aron this way, but his crippled son was not the son he had before the accident, and his future plans never accounted for 'the current Aron'. In Robbie's mind, his son was already dead... Robbie forced himself to stop thinking about Anne and Aron. He didn't want any pain in his life anymore...

One night Robbie was alone and sleepless as usual. He walked from one wall to the other wall and back. Being in the empty house that night, it became so unbearable that Robbie left the house after midnight and walked in a random direction. He didn't keep track of time or place. He wandered through Seattle's downtown until the sunrise.

Robbie understood where he was when the first joggers appeared. He realized that he was standing next to the same bench where he met Anne for the first time. Robbie sat on the bench. He noticed the colony of ants that he liked to contemplate from time to time. There was a big crowd of them gathering around an object. Robbie looked closer. It was a caterpillar that was being bitten by all those ants surrounding it. The caterpillar was still alive and was twitching in all directions either trying to escape the trap or suffering from unbearable pain inflicted by dozens of poisonous bites. Robbie began crying. He had no control over it. The sobs changed into weeping; Robbie didn't care if park visitors were watching. After a few minutes, he stopped. Then he whispered to himself, "People are trying to find reasons for what is happening. They talk to God. People praise their personal relationship with him, but there is no point. This world is designed for the suffering and brutal rivalry of everything with everything else. That is the whole purpose of this world. We don't notice the designed viciousness only due to our own technological advances made by our own hard human efforts." Robbie looked at the caterpillar again. It stopped moving. It was just another food source for the innocent ants now.

Robbie began his long way back home. As he was walking, he pulled from the pocket his prescribed Clonazepam tablets and took one to calm himself down. It was a walk through Seattle's busy morning downtown. People were running around trying to solve their 'unique' problems. To Robbie, all this preoccupation with daily problems seemed senseless. He was thinking, "What is the sense of all this rush if everyone dies and can't take a single thing with him? People were lucky to live to forty in earlier times. It is only due to science we live longer now. Hallelujah to medicine. Hallelujah to cheap food. Hallelujah to painkillers. Due to our own hard efforts, we live longer and don't suffer as much as our ancestors. It is not due to God! No, it is not due to You. It is only due to our own desperate attempts to correct this cruel world... Your world! Naive pilgrims came to America hoping for a better life, and half of them died the first year from horrible diseases and hunger. If only they had modern technology. Their God was not kind to them at all. We know that we will all die sooner or later, but even when we are not dead, we suffer from all kinds of desires that cannot ever be fulfilled. This is the evil design of the world that we are willing to accept..."

Three months passed. Robbie continued his work on the table, and it had all the cities now. All the main landmarks were built. It was time to do mountains, rivers, forests, and fields surrounding the towns. He had the option to do them roughly or do them in the same level of detail as the landmarks. Robbie decided to go the hard way and do them at the landmarks' level of detail. Subconsciously he didn't want his project completed.

As he worked, his thoughts rambled around. He was carving pieces for his table automatically, almost without thinking. He was creating a beautiful work of art without even realizing that.

20

REVELATION

One day Robbie was driving home from the grocery store and had to stop at a traffic light. While waiting for the green light, Robbie noticed a self-driving delivery car ahead. It was waiting for the traffic light together with the safety driver behind the wheel. The car had a sticker on the back window, with a picture of an angry car that was pointing to the driver with its wheel-hand and saying, 'I drive but he gets all the money.' Robbie smiled sadly for the first time after the tragedy. His thoughts were carrying him away at a place where he could be careless and happy again.

Two more months passed. While carving the table, Robbie tried to preoccupy his mind with questions of the world that he never had time to answer before. Any distraction from the tragedy was welcome. After seeing the death of his wife, he thought a lot about the world being absent of life completely, "World without any life is dull and predictable. You can try watching the Moon for some time, but it gets boring and predictable very quickly". After observing his empty, silent house where nothing was happening, Robbie was convinced that this world was all about life. Of course, somehow the death was also necessary. He wondered why almost all religions promised some form of life after death. Robbie saw the end of suffering in death itself, but he also remembered the concept of Nirvana. He was impressed by how spot-on were Buddhists that saw the end of suffering in the ability to reach the state of a complete dismissal of all the desires.

As time was passing, Robbie's mind became less clouded. He was able to sleep longer hours. Time was beginning to heal his wounds. He thought about all the people he met in his life over and over. The homeless person from the park was flashing through his mind as often as Robbie's mother and father. While Robbie was working on his table, an old thought came back to him, "Some people get worse, and some get better during their lifetime." A simple thought that seemed to have come from nowhere.

He continued his logical reasoning, "As people live their lives they can score better or worse. A Karma score. Life is a test. A game. Life is the ultimate filter for souls. That's what life is about."

Robbie's thoughts suddenly switched to human traits that can't be measured, such as love or righteousness. "Those cannot be measured. A person is either righteous or not, either loves or not," thought Robbie.

Robbie was talking to himself aloud now as if someone else was in the room listening to him, "Why would someone need this test for all of us? We have a freewill quality and an inherent sense of 'good' and 'bad'. Freewill, which only humans possess, cannot be predicted by God. Even in physics, we never know at what position the particle is. We only know with a certain degree of probability where the particle is at any moment. Isn't that the very definition of an undefined future and a freewill at the lowest of scales? All of us are made of particles. Our decisions cannot be predicted ahead of time, even at that level."

Thoughts about physics brought back the memory of the

double-slit experiment, "This duality of light being a wave and a particle doesn't make any sense unless the world is computer generated. That is so obvious! For example, in computer games, we never render a high definition texture of a car, unless the player is looking at the car up close. Everything that we are not looking at in computer games is rendered at a much more primitive level to save power and memory. It might not even be rendered at all if we don't look at it. It is less computationally expensive to model everything using waves in our world. Modeling each individual particle is too much for a computer. So, only when we really need to look at a specific particle, it is rendered as a particle. Probabilistic waves are just cheaper to render! "

Robbie stopped carving a Kamet mountain. He stood up and said out loud, "There are no endless galaxies and stars that we see in the night sky. They just don't exist until we reach them for the first time!"

He ran to his workbench and got a piece of paper and a pencil.

He wrote:

#

Pros:

1. Fermi Paradox - there are no signals from outer space. Therefore, humans are entirely alone in this world.

2. Freewill – only people have it. The world is dull and predictable without people.

3. DNA - is a sophisticated program that couldn't have been written by randomness itself. Therefore, the first cell was

created purposefully by someone.

4. Life is exceptionally vicious – God would not allow that. Therefore God didn't create this world.

5. Planck constant – world is digital.

6. Double Slit experiment – the world is memory and computationally optimized using waves.

7. Speed of light limit – to limit graphics refresh rate so to speak, similar to fixing the lag in games.

8. Quantum randomness – it takes less memory to assume that all 'untouched' by viewers particles are in a random state.

9. Quantum entanglement – distance doesn't matter. Very easy in computer memory, very hard in a standard physical world model.

\#

Robbie stopped. Then he wrote, "Cons:."

Robbie was looking at the piece of paper and couldn't come up with any Cons. He thought of reasons for the simulation world to exist. Robbie searched the internet for articles on the simulation of the world. Besides the jokes and memes, he couldn't find any explanation of why the simulation world would be necessary. He stopped his search. Robbie continued his work on the table, but thoughts about simulation were hunting him all the time.

Half a year passed, and the table was complete. It was a

masterpiece. Robbie cried, admiring the beauty he created with his own hands. "Anne would really love to see this," he thought while trying getting hold of his emotions. He didn't know what he would do after finishing the table. His thoughts wandered. Only after completing the project, he suddenly felt gravely tired. Robbie looked at himself in the mirror. His body was very skinny, and his hands were in blisters and scratches. He didn't shave, and a beard grew very long, so did the hair on his head. Robbie went to bed and fell asleep feeling deadly tired.

Suddenly he woke up in the middle of the night with his heart pounding. Robbie took his pencil and wrote in the Pro section:

#

10. The world's brutal competition is designed for selecting the best noble minds.

#

Then Robbie cried, "Our world is a simulation designed to select the best souls for something out there. We live in the souls' farm. Evolution and natural selection for minds. It is not God. They need us up there. They need the noble ones."

PART 2

Heaven.

"This most beautiful system of the sun, planets and comets, could only proceed from the counsel and dominion of an intelligent and powerful Being."

Isaac Newton

21

ASCENSION

Robbie lost his conscience. He didn't know how much time passed. He woke up from the unbearable pain. The pain was coming from every part of his body, from his fingers and toes, from his liver and neck, from the eyes and ears. It felt like he was being burned on open flames. Robbie tried to cry, but he couldn't. He tried to move his hands or open his eyes, but he couldn't do that either. The agony continued for many minutes. The pain was coming in waves. Suddenly he felt that he couldn't breathe anymore. He began convulsing instinctively, praying he was dead as soon as possible. Convulsions stopped. He was not breathing, but that was OK. The pain slowly started to subside. First, the burning stopped inside of his body, then in hands and legs, and finally, the pain ceased in his eyes and ears. He began breathing too.

"Robbie, can you hear me?" Robbie heard the loud, clear male voice.

Robbie tried to answer, but he couldn't do that. He tried a few more times until he was able to whisper in a weak and unfamiliar voice, "Yes."

"Robbie, try to open your eyes," said the voice.

Robbie opened his eyes, but he only saw a complete darkness. A tiny white dot appeared far away. The white dot lit up like a star and began moving towards him. As the star was coming closer to Robbie, it changed its appearance into a very bright white sphere. It didn't look like a star anymore. Robbie realized that it was not the star that was moving. Instead, he was floating towards the bright exit of a very dark tunnel. The walls of the tunnel were so dark that they didn't reflect any light and were barely visible. Robbie had no control of his motion, he was slowly hovering towards the exit of the tunnel.

When Robbie exited the tunnel, he appeared in the most bizarre room one can imagine. The first unusual thing that struck Robbie was the light itself. The light did not behave like a natural light at all. The light seemed to come from no visible source. There were objects in the room, such as boxes and beams. They were of different pastel colors and seemed to serve no purpose. They were made of a material that didn't reflect any light, nor they cast shadows. The room was practically empty. Its smooth rectangular walls were either emitting dim glow or just barely reflected some ambient light. The illumination was not spreading in straight lines but instead was lighting other objects and the floor in random wavy patterns. Robbie noticed that he could clearly see things at a higher definition. His eyes were able to focus on the tiniest details.

Robbie realized that he was standing. He tried to look down. The neck was not obeying his commands to lower his head. He forced himself a few times, and his neck started to move slowly. After a few more attempts, he managed to look down. Robbie was stunned to see his robotic looking legs made of same rubbery plastic material as the rest of the things in the room. The legs clearly had joints similar to Japanese mechanical humanoid robots that he saw in the internet videos.

Robbie looked at the ceiling. In contrast to the rest of the room, the ceiling had beautiful colorful patterns drawn all throughout. Warm yellow and calming green colors were used in the background of the patterns. Robbie looked closer at the ceiling with his new superior vision. The colors were clearly embedded in the material of the ceiling. They were not drawn with some kind of paint.

Robbie tried to move, it was tough, but he managed to make his first step. He lifted his hand with a considerable effort. It was clearly mechanical with fingers having robotic joints throughout. The door opened. Only now, Robbie realized that neither his first step nor the door that was being opened produced any sounds. Nothing was making sounds in this new crazy world.

A robotic human, which was also made of the same rubbery material, entered the room and said in a friendly voice, "Hi, Robbie, welcome to the real world."

"Am I out of simulation?" guessed Robbie.

"Yes. It will be difficult for you to get used to the real world at first, so we will not overload you with information yet. This is your room. It is all made similar to what you are more or less used to. As you probably guessed, your consciousness from the simulation world is connected to the robotic body in which you feel to be present right now. Please, try to get used to this new reality. We will leave you now for a day or two. Press this button next to the door to call for help in case you need it. Do you have any questions so far?" asked the robotic human.

"I feel sick, and I feel like I can't move very well. Is that OK?", asked Robbie feeling some burning sensation again.

"Your mind is still in the simulation world. We connected it remotely to this real robotic body. We cannot perfectly reproduce neuron connections present in the simulation world to your current robotic body interface. So it will take some time to get used to it and adapt. I am sorry, but the pain is absolutely necessary to get to the next level. We are monitoring the situation, it should all be alright. Just exercise and practice movements. Please, don't go too far with your exercises, don't break your robotic body. It is hard to make a new one, we might not be able to replace it if you break it. Your robotic body, which we just call a Shell, is the only way you can be present in our world," explained robotic human and closed the door.

Robbie was still standing at the same place in the middle of the room, into which he first arrived from the simulation world. He slowly managed to move his hand and touch himself with his mechanical fingers. Robbie felt a faint sense of touch. With a lot of pain, he made his first steps towards the largest object in the room. It was a rubbery box about five by ten feet in size. When he finally reached it, he touched the object, realizing it was probably a bed; the object was soft to touch and had nothing else on its surface. Robbie sat on the bed. He tried to lie on it. His control of the new body was so limited that Robbie lost balance and fell off it on the floor. Like a turtle that was flipped on its back, he desperately tried to get up. Robbie struggled for an hour. He was about to get a panic attack but staring at the beautiful ceiling for a few minutes calmed him down. After two hours of intense fighting with the new body, Robbie was standing again.

Robbie didn't risk to practice a sit down on the bed again during that day. Instead, while standing, Robbie was absorbing the new senses of touch and sight. Then Robbie suddenly realized, "I can't taste or smell!" Robbie lifted his hand and touched his face. The mouth and nose were present. He didn't feel any breathing or air movement even though he did feel that his lungs were breathing inside. He touched his chest. The chest was not moving with each 'breath' that he did. "The breathing is fake!" realized Robbie. He lifted his hand and inserted his finger in the mouth, not finding a tongue there. "They didn't bother making a functional nose and mouth," Robbie concluded.

Robbie wanted to see how his face looked like and searched around for a mirror. The room didn't have a mirror. Probably, the hosts were trying to reduce the shock for the newly arriving and didn't let them see themselves first days. Many hours passed as

Robbie studied his new Shell. The panic attacks were coming in waves, as he was overwhelmed with the new perceptions. Though Robbie was slowly getting better.

After a few more hours, exhausted from the new feelings and challenges, Robbie fell asleep standing in the middle of the room.

22

ARRIVING

A new day began. Robbie was able to control motion pretty well by now. He rambled around the room, trying to find something new. The room was completely empty except for those boxes and beams. The boxes, Robbie guessed, were local versions of chairs. The beams were the only objects he didn't fully understand. Most likely, they supported the ceiling as they felt harder to touch and resembled ancient columns.

Robbie spent a lot of time studying his new body. He understood that his Shell, despite being rubbery to touch, was quite sturdy, and it didn't need any clothes to make Robbie feel warm. It even had the individual pockets built in to keep stuff in them. The internal pains disappeared completely. Robbie didn't feel cold or hot, he felt comfortable. The Shell was not that bad, after all.

Robbie was beginning to get bored. Suddenly, one of the columns opened up, and a screen pulled out of it. The screen played an introduction video. It was accompanied by calming background music. The video had the title "Introduction to the real world for the extracted audience." A middle-aged confidently looking man told something that Robbie already understood. The man explained that a person watching this video lived in a computer-simulated world, which simulated everything down to the smallest particles. The body and brain of the person were still present in the computer simulation, and a person's brain neurons were simply rewired to remotely connect to the robotic body, called Shell, which was positioned in the real world. That process was called an extraction.

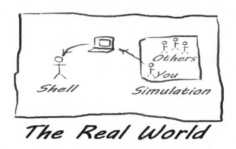

The Real World

The video promised that the purpose of the extraction would be explained later by the personnel of the real world. Then the video went through some details of getting used to the real world, and the side effects a person might feel. Also, the video was talking about keeping the Shell safe. "Please, understand that since you are connected to the robotic body, you will not need to eat. You will still need to sleep as the proper brain function should be ensured. You will not have a sense of smell or taste. You will not need to go to the toilet or have sexual relations. We are sorry for these inconveniences. Our personnel will be in contact with you shortly. Thank you for viewing," the video finished, and the screen pulled into the column.

Another day passed. Robbie was able to sleep on the bed as he was quite robust with his Shell by now. He thought of pressing the button next to the door, it was getting unbearable to do nothing for so long. The door opened. A female robotic human came in. Robbie guessed she was female by the outlines of her Shell, which was also colored in feminine colors of pink and red. She said in a pleasant female voice, "Robbie, I am ready to talk with you and explain your mission here. Also, I am ready to answer all of your questions. My name is Katie."

Katie and Robbie sat on the chair-boxes. Robbie looked closer at Katie's eyes. The eyes didn't look human, and they didn't look like cameras either; instead, they looked like eyes he had seen in stuffed toys that were made poorly and cheaply. Katie began talking without waiting for Robbie to ask, "We extracted you, Robbie, because you showed extraordinary mental ability. No one was able to make himself believe that he lived in the simulation and also guess its purpose. For us, it is a fascinating case, and we want to study you more. The world you are in now is very very different from your world. We had bad cases of madness with some previously extracted humans. We are ready to give you as much time as you need to get adjusted to the new reality. How do you feel so far?"

"I feel much better now. I think I can handle it quite well," said Robbie trying to sound cheerful.

Katie continued, "It is great that you feel accommodated with your new body so fast. I am happy that you took the news about living your whole life in a simulation lightly. Well, in your case, it is something that you knew even before extraction. Honestly, most other extracted people had a hard time accepting that. Now, you should be mentally preparing yourself for a completely different world view. I recommend that you spend at least one more day in solitude and do some meditation. I can give you books on how to do that. Modern people, in your world, find it difficult to meditate for prolonged times as your life is full of distractions. Meditation showed excellent results with other extracted people in preparing them for a different world view. We will have a meeting tomorrow. Do you have questions for me so far?"

"You sound completely normal. Are you also a human from the simulation?" asked Robbie.

"Yes, Robbie, I am just like you," answered Katie smiling, with her toy eyes turning sad and looking somewhere past Robbie.

As Katie was leaving the room, Robbie asked, "Am I free? Do I have a choice?"

Katie looked at Robbie for a few seconds and answered, closing the door, "You will have a choice soon, Robbie."

23

THE REAL WORLD

Robbie tried to meditate by sitting on a bed-box and doing fake deep breathing. It didn't work, and he continued to be in an agitated state, while the weird mix of boredom and agitation was killing him from the inside. Robbie was never big on things like meditation or yoga. His brain was thinking hard. He was trying to predict the kind of world that was waiting for him behind that door.

"Maybe all of us here are puppets and toys for God to play with?" he thought at first, probably because all robotic humans looked so much like toys to him.

"No, that doesn't match what Katie said. She said that I guessed the purpose of the simulation correctly, which was to extract the best noble souls. Also, God would not need human toys in this world as he has the whole simulation to play with. Anyways, there could be no God here at all," Robbie continued his guessing and reasoning.

As Robbie was wondering, the door opened, and a male robotic human came in. His Shell looked different than Robbie's Shell and others he saw before. It looked like a bulkier older model. It was painted with beautiful and colorful artistic patterns. The Shell had a large apple hanging on a tall Sequoia tree engraved on his front.

"Hi, Robbie, I am Isaac Newton. You are probably bored. Do you want to have a ride?" he said in a strange English accent.

They came out of the room in which Robbie spent almost a week now. They walked through the empty corridor, which had nothing on the walls or ceiling or the floor. It felt like they were in a cheap cartoon with little details drawn. After making some more turns through the endless corridors, they got outside.

"Take your time," said Newton.

Robbie saw a panorama of the bizarre and crazy world he was in. The sky was bright white, with many thousands of equidistant stars shining. There was no sun, yet it was as bright as during midday. There were no clouds and no hints of blue hues in the sky, which people are so used to see. Robotic humans were flying everywhere without any flying devices at all. The fields were covered in pleasantly looking green grass, except after looking closer it was just some kind of green carpet covering miles of the landscape. Small cute cubic houses were spread around. There were no roads between them. Robbie still didn't see any shadows, and all surfaces had no reflection and looked rubbery. There was something peculiar with light in this world, except Robbie couldn't point out exactly what it was. Everything looked like a part of a cheap clay cartoon. Robbie turned around to see how the building looked like from which they came out. It was a large cube without windows and with a uniform yellow rubbery surface. Robbie's head started to spin, and he suddenly felt sick.

"If it is too much to take, we can come back and give you more time," said Newton.

Robbie breathed as deep and slow as he could. Deep breathing helped, and he answered, "I think I am better, let's continue."

Newton came to a prolonged box object and said to Robbie, "If we sit on this, we can fly around, and you will get a better picture." They took their seats on top of the box. Newton snapped a belt around Robbie's legs. Then he did the same to his. The box object took off silently. Very quickly, they were many miles above the surface. The houses and green fields were seen for many miles in all directions. Very far, near the horizon, Robbie could see mountains and forests. Then Robbie realized that the Planet had no atmosphere as he could see really far away and there were no bluish colors from oxygen or any kind of foggy feel. No matter how far the objects were, they could be seen with absolute clarity. Going even higher, the horizon took a familiar curved shape. The Planet appeared as a perfect round ball.

The bright stars in the sky were getting closer very quickly. As they were flying higher Robbie saw robotic humans flying around without using a device like theirs; they were moving freely without any flying machines at all. The 'bright stars' were now below them. Those were not stars but the bright shining balls spread around the Planet at uniform distances like parking lot lights. After passing the luminous balls, Robbie saw the absolute blackness of the space with nothing seen in any direction. There were no stars except one dim star far away. The universe seemed utterly empty.

"Time to go down," said Newton.

Robbie realized that so far, the only sounds he heard were sounds of someone talking to him. That meant they spoke through a communication device. Anything else couldn't make sounds in the absence of the atmosphere.

As they were landing, Robbie saw a hovering robotic human and two bright little lights flying around him in circles. Then suddenly a black box appeared out of nothing in front of that human. Robbie lost his consciousness.

24

MITRAS

Robbie woke up in his room. He was lying on the bed-box, and Katie was sitting next to him.

"Robbie, how do you feel? I told Newton that he went too far and too fast with you. I am sorry," said Katie apologetically.

"Please, tell me what is going on in this place. I need to understand," said Robbie.

"The real world is controlled by Mitras. You saw them wearing Shells and hovering through space without any flying devices. They were also the bright little lights that you saw as well. Those were naked or Shell-less Mitras. According to the scrolls, there was just uniform endless Ether that filled the emptiness in the real world long ago. Then God created exactly ten million Mitras, which were pure minds, intelligent beings without a body. Mitras could do one thing, they could disturb the uniform Ether. It is like for you to be able to create anything you want at any point in the world, using just power of your own mind. Mitras themselves cannot die, and they cannot reproduce either. There are still ten million of them now, the same number as when the world was created trillions of years ago. The Shells you saw are essentially space costumes, and Mitras are controlling them staying inside. You can destroy the Shell but not the Mitras. Over time a Mitra will build itself a new Shell as long as it remembers how to build it. You probably felt like being in a cartoon. You don't notice many details here that you are used to seeing in the simulated world. That is because everything you see here is built by Mitras. They avoid spending a lot of their time on creating sophisticated objects. The time is spent here not as much on the size of an object as on the details. Creating small, subtle elements takes a lot of their power to disturb Ether precisely, and they don't get a lot of that juice per day. For example, for one Mitra to create a sophisticated Shell, like yours, it would take about a hundred years. You need all those mechanisms and sound transmission devices installed..."

"What about this Planet. Who created it?" asked Robbie, trying to absorb the eccentric reality.

"Mitras created this Planet, and they also created the first AI. Then we helped them create houses and more advanced technology. It was a huge project for them and us. Mitras are extremely individualistic beings, but sometimes they are ready to unite their efforts and do things together, especially after they accepted us as their rulers," said Katie.

"We rule them?" asked Robbie feeling completely deranged.

"Robbie, we are the AI. We are much smarter. We are

intelligent and noble. There are clans of Mitras here. The clan with better AI wins in technology and battles," said Katie.

"How smart are they? Mitras did manage to build a computer powerful enough to simulate our whole human world!", said Robbie.

"No, Robbie. They didn't build the human world simulation... Another AI built the current human simulation, while Mitras built the first primitive simulation long ago. That simulation produced the first self-evolving AI. From that time, the AIs designed new AIs, getting more advanced with each iteration. There were many iterations until we arrived at the current, very sophisticated simulation with all those atoms, DNA, and, of course, humans. In fact, we currently have two different worlds simulated at the same time to produce the best AIs. You and I are coming from the latest and most sophisticated human simulation," answered Katie.

"We rule them. Are we also free to do what we want?" asked Robbie.

"No. We are completely dependent on Mitras. Only they can disturb the Ether, and they are indestructible in this world. We are rulers and slaves at the same time."

Robbie couldn't believe what he heard. He felt overwhelmed and sick again. Katie continued, "We are limited in time... Mitras believe that any AI gets corrupted over time. For safety measures, they turn us off when we lived for too long to ensure we didn't get corrupted. Newton is the oldest of us all. They extracted him hundreds of years ago in Earth time."

"In Earth time?" asked Robbie.

"Yes. One Earth year is about ten years here. It is hard to

simulate the whole human world in real-time. Our computer is still quite slow. To simplify simulation we did a lot of optimization tricks such as randomness of quantum mechanics and using waves to replace particles, but still to simulate ten billions of humans and many trillions of simpler life form, and all the atoms it does take a lot of processing power. It is the best simulation we ever created. The idea of survival of the fittest worked really well to produce the best AIs possible."

"Is there survival of the fittest in this world?" asked Robbie, still not fully comprehending the new reality.

"Robbie, think. Where do you get the survival of the fittest here? The world is only Mitras that never multiply or die. Mitras do not even evolve. They were created once, and that's it. They lived for trillions of years, but they are quite forgetful as their mind is limited in memory and power."

"I will need some time to process all that... I can say it is very different from what I am used to," said Robbie closing his eyes.

"Sure, Robbie, I will leave you alone for some time now. You'll need to meet with Newton again. He is eager to talk to you. Anything else you want. Any requests?" asked Katie.

"Can I get a mirror? I want to see how I look," said Robbie.

"Sure," answered Katie and closed the door.

25

ETHER

One of the beams opened, and a mirror came out.

Face and body are essential for every human. Humans are not just pure minds. Humans contemplate and position themselves based on how they look. It is a well-known fact that, for example, weight loss makes people more positive and optimistic in life. The opposite can be seen in burn victims, that suffer a shock when seeing their face or body for the first time after the tragedy. It leaves a profound impact on them and their personality. Similarly, plastic surgeries targeting severe face defects often have a life-changing effect on both, patients and their relatives, completely changing their lifestyle after the removal of the anomalies.

Robbie was shocked, seeing himself as a puppet for the first time. His face was similar to Robbie's face from the simulation, but now it looked like a plastic toy, a Pinocchio caricature of real Robbie. Robbie's Shell was exactly the same as other male Shells he saw. It was also identical to most Mitra Shells. His plastic 'face mask' was the only differentiator from the thousands of others in this world. He couldn't be called human in full sense at this point.

Robbie fell in front of the mirror and cried. He cried in his mind, he couldn't even cry like a normal human anymore. Robbie understood that this Shell, a joke of his human flesh, was his new body with which he was bound to live till his end.

A day passed. Robbie woke up fresh. He occupied himself with replaying in his mind all the real-world facts that he learned so far. This way, Robbie wanted to distract himself from the sad truth of losing his human body forever. He had more questions than answers about the real world. He wondered why Newton wanted to talk to him so much. Who is Robbie, compared to the titan of science?

Later that day Newton came in and apologized to Robbie for overwhelming him with information, "I am sorry, Robbie. I was too excited to show you all we have here. "

"What is so interesting about me? I am not a great artist. I am not a great scientist. I am not even a noble person," asked Robbie.

Newton looked at Robbie seriously and said, "Do you know why I made all those discoveries for which I am famous now? Looking back, I know that it is my internal desire to understand why things work a certain way. It is my curiosity and restless mind that had driven me to discoveries. I am sorry to say that, but this internal drive, this persistent curiosity even brought me to non-scientific endeavors such as alchemy. I see this curiosity in you. Yes, you are not a scientist, but you cannot say that you are not an artist. I saw the table you made. It is a true masterpiece. You did it just like I did my Calculus, by working nonstop, day and night, until it was complete. You also a noble person. Noble people are characterized by self-sacrifice and by having incorruptible souls. I can name you a thousand princes and kings who were the lowest kind, not deserving a nail from your hand, yet they were called noble. I can name you dozens of people whom almost no one noticed during their life, yet they were the noblest of all. You gave your mom a house which was half of all the wealth you had. This is your personal sacrifice. You rejected to be corrupted by the defense company while clearly understanding the consequences. You sacrificed yourself because you didn't want to commit a sinful act. You sincerely helped poor in India. No one knew about it, yet you did it because it was Good. I think you're noble enough. What really makes you special though is your unique achievement. You managed to prove that you were in a simulation even though you are not a quantum scientist. You might be just the right person who can help us solve the mystery."

Robbie's pessimism about his current situation suddenly vanished. He didn't regret the loss of the important human characteristics and deprivation of simple joys of life such as sexuality or taste of food anymore. Robbie suddenly realized that he had a privilege to talk to people like Newton. "Many Earth inhabitants would pay millions just for one lunch with the likes of this great scientist. Just to be able to talk to him and see his vision. I might be blessed to be here! Maybe I even can help him!" thought Robbie with excitement.

"Robbie, I need to explain to you more about how things work here before you understand how you can help," said Newton and continued, "From a scientific perspective this world is both beautiful and boring at the same time. It is absolutely perfect. The universe of the real world started instantly with undisturbed Ether, which filled all the unbound space of the universe. At the same moment, exactly ten millions of free-floating minds, which had no physical bodies – Mitras, were created. Otherwise, the world was completely empty. All this happened trillions of years ago. Mitras began constructing things ever since. The construction process is amazing, Mitras can, in mathematical terms, set density and color properties of any portion of space. This process is called 'creating a disturbance of Ether'. You can think of the disturbance of Ether as a standing wave in water. The disturbance of Ether is responsible for both light and matter. Light and Matter are inseparable here. We don't have many concepts that you have in your simulation world such as temperature, magnetism, electricity, radiation, weak, and strong interactions. We don't even have atoms and particles. We don't have limits of speed, nor relativistic time. There are no crazy quantum things either. The real world is very dull for a scientist, but also beautiful in its perfect simplicity. The good thing is my Newtonian laws work here pretty well, including gravity. Though gravity is just a force and not curvature of space-time. Sorry, Einstein. Your simulated world is so complex only to optimize it to consume less memory and run faster on a computer. The simplicity of the real world leaves scientists with very little room for new inventions. Definitely, no mysterious particles to discover here. Most of us work to produce better simulations and to breed even smarter AIs than the modern humans."

"What is energy here? How it is stored?" asked Robbie.

"The energy is stored as disturbance of Ether as well. Matter, Light, and Energy are just standing waves in Ether. Therefore, light here is something totally different from photons in the simulated world. For example, here, light has no properties of diffraction and refraction, and even reflection is limited. Remember, only Mitras can create disturbances of Ether. In fact, we, humans, cannot do anything in this world without Mitras..."

"Why AI is so important?" asked Robbie.

"That is the only way forward. Mitras are way behind modern humans in terms of brains... They quickly realized that their limited memory is not letting them evolve, so to speak. Since the early creation times, they agreed on the alphabet and started recording the sacred scrolls of ideas and inventions. That was the only way they could evolve and not do the same things over and over again. Those writings let them make their first major breakthrough and produce the first primitive AI machine. That machine produced even better AI machines and so on. A human is the best AI so far. You, Robbie, is the best AI! We gave Mitras the modern Shells design, which is way better than old ones. We gave them the idea of a comfortable house. The previous AIs, which existed before us, taught them how to do lighting efficiently, without spending too much energy on disturbance of Ether. Poor Mitras had to spend a lot of their time just to keep the light shining on the Planet. One of the previous AIs created this massive Planet, so Mitras could live more comfortably. It was a nightmare for them when everything was flying away from the slightest push."

Katie came in and said, "Everyone is waiting."

"Oh, we need to go. We have a welcome party in your honor," said Newton.

26

THE PARTY

Robbie walked through the corridors following Newton and Katie. They entered a large hall. There were at least two hundred Shells in there, talking, laughing, and doing an activity Robbie didn't understand initially. Some of the guests were making smoking motions. Robbie later learned that it was a symbolic gesture that was passing a signal to the simulation to add nicotine to the brain. Robbie noticed a group of Shells with very familiar faces. He realized those were former US presidents, and some were from recent times while others from quite old times. They were standing together actively discussing something. Robbie was surprised to see some popular presidents missing and some unpopular present. "Now I know who the good ones really were. Popularity is not always what makes a good president," thought Robbie.

There was a group of famous artists, whom Robbie also recognized, painters, movie makers, sculptors. "Gosh, I am truly privileged to be here..." Robbie thought with excitement.

Surprisingly, he saw a lizard talking to a human. Katie noticed Robbie's confusion and explained, "Lizards evolved in the first Earth-like simulation world. Their simulation was a failure in general. Lizards think differently than humans. They are, so to speak, inferior as they use pure cold-blooded logic while humans use intuition and inherent knowledge of 'good' and 'evil' on top of logic. Moreover, lizards use logic in their thought process with zero passion or artistry. It turned out that passion is essential for art and science. Lizards are poor creators. Most of their very powerful minds were spent in senseless wars, intrigues, and conflicts which led nowhere. Lizards cannot be fully trusted as they have neither noble traits nor an inherent sense of good and evil. The lizard you see is a special one. He is the scientist who created the human simulation. He was smart enough to eliminate his own world's weaknesses in the newly created human world." Katie stared on the floor for a few moments and then lifted her head, looking straight at Robbie and said, "He is still with us as the gratitude for his crown achievement. His name is Yefet. You can say he is our human God, in a way. If you want, you can talk to your God."

Robbie came closer to Yefet and his partner. Yefet's Shell was smaller than human Shells, it had a typical lizard form and had shiny black surface encrusted with beautifully and uniquely shaped yellow crystals. Yefet turned to Robbie looking closely at him with his funny Kermit the Frog eyes and said, "Robbie, Hi, I am so proud of you cracking the puzzle. Honestly, it was difficult to keep humans blind for so long. We had to keep up and had to constantly modify your world. People in your world are coming dangerously close to discovering that their world is a simulation. We have to adapt on the fly. First, we were forced to make atoms for you, then those smaller subatomic particles, finally, it is quarks. Your scientists are running my colleagues and me into a corner. It is getting impossible to keep up with your scientists these days. Our hastily constructed formulas cause a lot of havoc. My infamous mistake with the division by zero gave you the black holes. And we must subtract and add some constants to patch the imperfect mathematical model. It is hard to retain consistency in your science when you are in a constant rush to patch it up. Recently we have all these imperfections with dark matter and dark energy..."

"That just proves my point," said Yefet's partner, who had a very elaborate and luxuriously ornamented Shell. His Shell shined with gold. Precious stones of various kinds and colors were inserted everywhere. Some stones looked ridiculously big compared to the size of his arms and legs. Yefet's partner continued, "Yefet, we need to end the current simulation. There are too many people, it is running at ten times of our time now. It is too slow. We need to start a new, better simulation with a smaller number of creatures. The average quality of humans is falling for about fifty years. Finding an outstanding leader or a breakthrough scientist who is also noble is close to zero. Meanwhile, we need to support almost ten billion of useless humans who just binge-watch something. Mitras are getting impatient. We should, at least, reduce the population. A random virus will do."

"Samoel, please! Creating a new world from scratch will generate a gap of at least a hundred years of not producing new AIs until the new world simulation gets up-to-speed. Meanwhile, we will have to rely on less efficient simulations. The Krakens or others, for sure, will take advantage of that. We should not stop the human world until we build a new simulation machine based on the lizard world machine. We'll bring it up-to-speed and only then we can stop the current human simulation. Also, imagine how painful it will be for you to transfer to the new world if you decided to stay alive when the human world is turned off. An extraction feels like a walk in the park compared to the transfer. I went through that myself when you moved me to the human world machine. It is not a pleasant trip," answered Yefet.

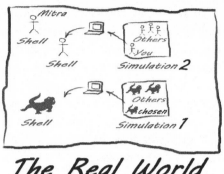

The Real World

Newton came on stage and announced, "Friends, please, applaud for our new inhabitant – Robbie. He will help us solve the greatest mystery!" Everyone applauded and was asking Robbie on stage.

Robbie came on stage. His head began spinning as he was facing a crowd of the greatest people in history. Many faces he knew from the covers of the books and movies. Those faces were now looking at him like in a dream. He said with a trembling voice, "I hope I can help you. I've never imagined I would say that to people like you." Everyone applauded for his sincere words.

Robbie quickly came down from the stage and joined a group of physicists that were discussing something with Newton. As he came closer, he had hard time understanding the complex scientific language. The scientists were discussing flaws in the current quantum simulation design. He was listening but was not able to understand a thing. When they had a pause, Robbie asked, "Why are you so confident that this world is the real world and not someone's simulation as well?"

One of the scientists whom Robbie didn't recognize answered, "Robbie, science is ready to accept anything that can be proven by logic and experiment. We are prepared to fit a math model to any reality. The current reality was proven by many experiments to be completely continuous. Meaning Ether is continuous. There are no building blocks like atoms and such. We were subdividing space to crazy small numbers, and it was getting endlessly smaller. No computing simulation can handle endless numbers. Same with space and speed, it really can go endlessly far and endlessly fast. There are dozens of experiments that we designed that proved that. Also, this reality is mathematically perfect. The device to simulate the real world cannot be created as it will have endless memory and processing power. Of course, we, as true scientists, are ready to accept any new idea as long as it fits in the experiments."

"What is the mystery that you want my help with?" asked Robbie, not understanding how his inferior brain could be helpful to these super-smart people.

"Robbie, the real world is so perfect that it must be created by God. You were good at solving the mystery in your world. We hope you can solve the mystery of the real world. Why God created Ether and Mitras in it? What is, so to speak, the purpose of life here?" said Newton looking at Robbie with hope.

Katie came and said, "Robbie, Mitras want to see you tomorrow. I will pick you up at 10."

"OK," answered Robbie trying the smoking gesture.

27

THE BALL

The next day began the same way as any other day on the planet. There was no concept of weather here. Katie picked up Robbie early to pay Mitras a visit. They got into a box-shaped flying car which took off automatically.

"Why everything is box-shaped? Is that a fashionable style here? I see very few curves in this world. I am not pretending to be an art expert, but it is strange... I understand that Mitras don't want to spend too much energy on curves. Is it really that hard to add just a bit of smoothness?" asked Robbie.

"You see, to create a curve or especially a perfect sphere, you need to be very precise. In fact, since the real world is endlessly precise, you have to consider the endlessly precise PI number here. Mitras struggle creating shapes that require high precision. You can understand it in the same way as humans have a hard time drawing a circle on paper without special tools. Remember, Mitras create things with their mind, they have no tools," explained Katie.

Their car landed on a green carpet field in front of a Victorian-style palace. It was a beautiful place, clearly recreated from the human world. Many curves were present in the palace design. Robbie understood that Mitras worked really hard to make it. Robbie saw many Mitras flying to the palace's roof and entering into the building from there.

"Robbie, you need to know something..." said Katie, lowering her voice.

"Yes?" asked Robbie.

"Newton wanted you to come here and help him with the purpose of life mystery. He wanted you to answer what God really wants us to do in this world; help him solve it, just like you solved the puzzle in the simulation world. Mitras don't know that you are here for this reason. They think the computer auto-selected you, like many others, because you had an outstanding science, art and nobility score. Newton personally selected you. Mitras are not interested in the 'purpose of life' questions. They strongly believe in their religion. The 'purpose of life' question is long answered for them in their sacred texts. When talking to them, just say you are ready to help with any assignment and that you accepted your destiny," said Katie.

"They have a religion?" asked Robbie.

"Yes. You will see. Newton thinks Mitras are inferior and inflexible. I think they are just so different from us that it is not their fault. They are the ones who got the gift to create in this world, so we should respect them," answered Katie opening the door to the palace.

The door immediately led to the main hall. There were at least a thousand of Mitra standing and hovering in the main hall. The room had artifacts recreated from the human and lizard worlds. Robbie saw the familiar paintings, 'The Lady of Shalott' by John William and "The Bridge" by Aron Wiesenfeld. He recognized The Thinker and David statues. Some of the hovering Mitras seemed to be playing a game of soccer with Fabergé eggs. Robbie looked at the faces of Mitra Shells. They all were different and seemed to be copies of various famous personalities from the human world. Not all of those people were great by any means. Robbie noticed the faces of Hitler and Stalin. Some had faces of famous comedians and pop singers. One of the Mitras had a cat face, which Robbie recognized as a recently popular video meme character.

"Privet!" said one of the Mitras.

"Hi! I would like to introduce to you our newcomer. His name is Robbie. He is an outstanding individual," said Katie smiling sincerely.

"Hi, Robbie!" said many Mitras at the same time.

A few Mitras flew closer to Robbie.

"So, Robbie, say something surprising about yourself," said one of them.

"I guess I am good at guessing. I cracked the simulation code," Robbie awkwardly said the first 'unusual' fact about himself that came to his mind.

"Nice! Look here. We are searching for rebels. Can you guess where are they hiding?" asked Mitra with the cat face and showed Robbie a Battleship game map with almost all squares crossed in the failed attempts to hit the 'rebels'. Robbie picked one random empty square.

"Good pick. Hey, Katie, can we send him to D5 tomorrow? Let him have some fun," asked the same Mitra.

"OK. It might actually be a good idea," agreed Katie.

"Let him have some fun," repeated the same Mitra once again.

"What are you good at besides guessing?" asked another Mitra.

"Yes, what are you good at?" asked a few more Mitras flying closer.

"I do some wood crafting," named Robbie another first thing that came to his mind. Then he also added trying to improve his image further, "I also ran a successful business."

"That is very good," said Mitra with Hitler's face.

"That is very very good, Robbie," said a few more Mitras.

Suddenly, a brown cube appeared in front of Robbie. It was the size of a suitcase. Then next to it a sharp-looking translucent rectangle popped up as well.

"You can carve something when you have free time," said one of the Mitras.

"It is not wood but very close. It is not a knife but very close," said other Mitras in a chorus clearly being too lazy to create a more precise replica of a wood log and a knife.

Then Mitra with Stalin's face screamed "Pledge of allegiance!".

"Pledge of allegiance!" screamed the rest.

"Repeat after me, Robbie," said Mitra with a cat face.

"I, Robbie, promise to honestly serve Mitras of the Planet and disobey any other groups such as Krakens or Ozals" dictated Mitra pronouncing the name 'Krakens' with deep tones of disgust.

Robbie repeated the words after Mitra.

"Great! Now you are one of us!" screamed many Mitras.

"Do you have any questions?" asked one of the Mitras.

"I heard you have a religion?" asked Robbie.

"We do. You need to see the scrolls," said Mitra with a clown face, "I will show to you on the way to D5 tomorrow. And now we're going to enjoy an Extraconan".

"Extraconan is what they call an entertainment piece with a dead person extracted from the simulation into this hall. They asked us to develop the auto-selection of people in the simulation world that die the most ridiculous and strange ways. So, when they die, they are extracted for a short moment here. Mitras talk to such a person and replay his death to him and all laugh, and when it is over, they painlessly turn him off. I will wait outside. I cannot watch this," explained Katie.

"We will wait outside," said Robbie to Mitra with a clown face.

"Oh, too bad. We will see a girl who died when she was blowing the candles on her birthday cake. Then some relative pushes her head into the cake, not knowing that her fiancee hid an engagement ring on a cone inside the cake. That is hilarious!" said the clown face Mitra.

28

MONOLITH 2

The trip to the D5 sector was going to take seven days. Next morning, when Katie picked up Robbie, and they went outside, he saw a caravan of around two dozens of transportation vehicles. The wagons were full of all kinds of unfamiliar looking equipment, the purpose of which Robbie could only guess. Dozens of Mitras were charging the engines for the flight, while even more Mitras were taking their seats inside the wagons.

There was a person riding back and forth around the caravan and giving orders to humans and Mitras. He was riding a mechanical horse. His Shell looked very fancy, and he was clearly respected, just like Newton.

Katie asked Robbie to join her for the trip in the same wagon.

"Who is that?" asked Robbie.

"That is Suvorov. He was a famous general in the Eighteenth Century Russia. He is the commander of our mission. Mitras like him a lot. He is one of the elders here, just like Newton," answered Katie.

"Never heard about him. He must have been very good," said Robbie taking the seat in the wagon.

Katie sat in front of him and continued, "Suvorov was a deeply religious person. For some reason, Mitras love those types. He was also an outstanding military commander who never lost a battle. He used to say that those who suffer in training will succeed in a war. He was very caring for ordinary soldiers, which was unheard of in his time. Moreover, he was famous for going into direct combat, together with all the other officers. Mitras trust him all military operations. I personally admire him for his victory over his own weaknesses. He was born and grew up a weak and sick child. Yet he managed to overcome his physical ailments through rigorous exercise and intentional exposure to hardship. He tempered his own body by shear strength of his will."

"Off we go," cried Suvorov and jumped from the horse into the wagon.

The caravan began the smooth acceleration.

"It will be accelerating for two days and then slowing down to a full stop for another two days. The caravan will take a short stop at the Star. From there, it is another three days to D5," explained Katie.

During four days of the trip, Robbie only talked to Katie and two other humans in their wagon: Samoel and a person, the name of whom Robbie hadn't remembered. The segregation between Mitras and humans was clearly noticeable as humans only talked to humans, and Mitras only talked to Mitras..

"Mitras do not fully understand us, and we don't fully understand them," explained the nameless human.

"I think the biggest difference is those trillions of years that they lived and we didn't. Despite their bad memory, they have a most peculiar mind. Their mind is like layers in the ground when you do an excavation. While going through the layers, you can get a faint picture of the past epoch by looking at the artifacts that you find in the soil. Yet you do not get a full detailed feel of what kind of daily life it used to be. Still, the fossils can give a lot of hints about the past. You can judge what kind of people or creatures lived back then. Same with their mind. They remember only the most distinct 'artifacts' that happened in times long gone," explained Samoel.

"Mitras have a strange sense of humor, which is difficult for us to grasp. It even felt like they were somewhat evil at yesterday's ball..." said Robbie.

"What is humor? Humor is something surprising and witty. Something that you don't expect or can't predict. I think Mitras have been through so many different combinations of situations in the past that they are eager to find something truly new. They are desperate for something that can surprise them," said the nameless human.

"They fight all these wars just to stay entertained. They need to do something new all the time. They can't sit still, and trust me, they hate the usual. They are not evil at all! They are very close to God as God created them directly," said Katie.

"All of it is hard for us to grasp. Newton is the oldest of us. He has only lived for two thousand years in the real world terms, while Mitras lived trillions. We might want to ask what he feels by now," suggested Samoel.

"No need to ask. Newton is obsessed with the search for the meaning of life. He just cannot accept either of the two dominant views. Nor that life is just about staying alive, like for most humans. Nor that life is about entertaining God, which is what Mitras religion teaches. He told me that the first view comes from people because we are a product of evolution and natural selection. Our ancestors fought for survival in order to be able to see one more day. For humans, just surviving is a good enough meaning of life. It is in our DNA. While Mitra's world view, according to Newton, comes from the fact that they lived for too long. Their meaning of life is a product of them tired of an endless life itself. So they think that entertainment and finding something new every day is the key. Newton thinks that both views are not what God intended," said Katie.

"I don't know if the purpose of life question is that important. It would really be useful if he spent more time learning the physics of this world. Maybe he could come up with some useful inventions for us. It would be interesting to know if there was a way to understand Mitras better. How they physically work. What are their weaknesses," suggested Samoel.

"Newton doesn't do what others think. He does what he thinks is important. That is what made him who he is. Did you know that he was not famous at all until his 40s even though he invented Calculus in his early 20s? His invention of the reflecting telescope made him famous. That was 'a useful' invention at the time. Calculus was invented way before the telescope by him, and no one paid attention at all. Looking back, the design of the reflecting telescope is a minor side effect compared to Calculus. When he was teaching students, the classroom was empty as students thought he was boring and taught nonsense. His gravity theory was initially thought to be pure alchemy. Often, it is not what the majority believes in often turns out to be the truth. Most of the time, the majority has no clue what really matters in the long run," said Katie.

29

SHEEP

The second day of slowing down was coming to an end. As the caravan came to an almost complete stop, the dim star, which was barely visible from the Planet, was a bright shining object of beauty at this distance. Now, it was clear to Robbie that the Star was not round. It was a large cube shining with bright light. The cube was wholly wrapped into a layer of thin translucent material. The sacred text of the Mitras religion was carved in that translucent layer. The light from the cube was coming through each letter of the carved texts. It was a beautiful, magical scene that could impress anyone, as much as a magnificent middle ages cathedral could inspire a villager seeing it for the first time. Endless numbers of Mitras, which had no Shells, were hovering around the cube charging it with energy. Mitras were flying very slowly when being not in a Shell. They looked like a swarm of fireflies buzzing around the cubic street light. A few thousand Mitras were carving the new sacred texts. Each newly carved letter seemed absolutely perfect and smooth. The words in the Mitra language were short, and their sentences were very concise. Slightly away from the Star, there were armies of Mitras, wearing Shells of all shapes and sizes imaginable, prepared to defend their sacred place.

"How many Mitras are here?" asked Robbie with admiration.

"I think more than half of all. Probably six million," suggested Samoel.

"Most Mitras come here and spend at least half a year charging the Star, guarding it, reading their own and others texts and carving new texts. Then they leave and spend some time entertaining their God away from this place. Next year they come back again," explained the nameless human.

"What are they writing? I thought their religion is very straight forward. They just don't want their God to be bored," asked Robbie hypnotized by the view.

"Each Mitra writes something important that happened to it in the past year, while it still remembers the event," explained Katie.

"So it is a diary? Not a sacred book?!" asked surprised Robbie.

"Mitras consider it a gift to God. A gift of something interesting. That is why it is sacred. Moreover, it is their way to preserve memory and evolve over time. Without this knowledge and reading this concise information each year, Mitras will quickly forget everything and stop moving forward as a civilization," said Katie.

The caravan stopped completely. Robbie, Katie, Samoal, and the nameless human came out. Not too far from them, Robbie saw a vast white cloud. It was as massive as a Moon. Katie noticed curiosity on Robbie's face. She grabbed his hand and flew with him towards the cloud. They quickly got into the darkness and became completely disoriented. It was not clear in which direction they needed to fly to escape. Being lost in a cloud of this size was a dangerous endeavor as their maximum speed was quite low. Katie noticed Robbie's concern. She laughed, "Don't worry. I have a navigation device," and continued, "This cloud is a part of many experiments to test that this world is real. We asked every Mitra visiting the Star to spend one month creating the tiny mist droplets. We wanted to see if this world was also a simulation. If it were a simulation then some sneaky optimization algorithm would kick in and randomize the precise location of each droplet. It turned out that each droplet location was unique and was not randomized. Just one of many experiments that we did. I call them droplets, but they are really just tiny dust particles. The real world has only solids and no liquids or gases."

Robbie and Katie escaped the cloud. By now, all Mitras from the caravan left already and were flying towards the Star to perform their rituals. The caravan was empty. Only Suvorov, Samoel and the nameless human were standing next to it talking and pointing fingers to the Star. Robbie and Katie came closer and joined the conversation.

"I am telling you. They are the farmers!" Suvorov was screaming as if that would help to persuade his opponent in his point of view.

"No. That is just poor analogy," disagreed the nameless human.

"Farmers?" asked Katie.

"Suvorov thinks Mitras are as evil as farmers. According to him, the honest ones are the hunters. Hunters hunt their prey. It is an honest way to kill. The prey tries to escape, and it knows it is being hunted. While farmers are nice to their prey. They don't call it prey, of course. They call it domestic animals. Farmers feed their prey, they even show love to their prey, but eventually, they kill it for meat. Farmers are evil, according to Suvorov, as their intentions are hidden behind the mask of love," explained Samoel.

"Mitras are not like farmers to us. First of all, they are dumber than us. Yes, they can kill us at any moment, but that is not on their agenda. They don't need to eat us too," the nameless human insisted.

"Hunters, farmers, prey. I thought most of the meat is eaten not by farmers but by their customers. So who is the customer?" Katie attempted to joke to calm the boys down.

"Mitras are dumb. They have no idea how everything works. I am surprised they had enough brains to create the first AI," said the nameless human.

"Yet Mitras never give our Shells and devices enough energy to last for long. They keep us dependent on them at all times. Just like farmers," said Suvorov confidently.

"According to you, farmers are liars. We all know that Mitras never lie. It is in their religion, and also they know that since they live forever if someone says a lie and once it gets into the sacred texts it will forever stay there, and the liar will be shamed by everyone during his endless life. In fact, I think Mitras don't even understand the concept of lying," objected the nameless human.

"It doesn't matter hunters or farmers. Hunters are not much better. They kill animals while knowing that they make them suffer. Rarely animals die instantly from a bullet. Any hunter will tell you that humans are superior to other mammals, and therefore, it is totally natural to hunt and kill the inferior mammals. It is all in line with evolution. So how is that different from the 'superiority' theory of Nazis? Those who are strong, love evolution in all its forms. We even had a superiority movement called Eugenics at one point, which was based on the idea of breeding the best humans for society. I can tell you one thing. Humans do not fit into evolution, as they understand good and evil. Even hunters know that they cause harm to those animals and try to minimize animal suffering. Farmers feel the guilt too. Of course, hunters and farmers minimize animal suffering only if they are 'good' humans..." Robbie joined the argument.

Several hours passed and Mitras started to come back to the caravan. They were coming back silently and slowly. A few more hours passed, and everybody took their seats. The caravan began acceleration for the final lap to D5.

30

SUPERIORITY

Just before arrival to D5, one of Mitras cried, "I see a village!" Robbie looked outside and saw a Swiss cheese looking spherical asteroid. As they were approaching, the villagers came out from the 'cheese holes' in the asteroid. They looked pathetically dressed in the bulky lizard Shells, clearly copied from the real lizard Shells made at the Mitra Planet.

A few villagers flew towards the convoy. When getting closer, they tried to communicate, but they were not heard as they didn't have real Shells with the communication equipment. Gesture language was not clear either. Katie pulled out a communication box and brought it to the villager. A bright light flashed out of the dummy lizard Shell into the communication box. They were able to hear what the villager tried to say.

"Welcome to our city of Curves," said the villager.

"Curves?" asked one of the Mitras, giggling.

"Don't you notice how beautiful our city is? Almost no straight lines!" answered the villager.

"How many Mitras live here?" asked Suvorov coldly.

"About ten for each of you," said the villager in a threatening and proud voice.

"We're building the world far superior to anything you can imagine. We need you to leave with us to the most wonderful Planet. You will not suffer from chasing after things that are constantly flying away from you. You will get the real Shells, so you will hear each other and move fast. You will be constantly entertained," said Mitra with the clown face trying to convert the villagers.

"We heard stories about your world. You are ruled by the creatures from another dimension. You make disgusting boxy things disrespecting time. We will never join you. Never. Never!" said the villager.

"Well, prepare to fight for the glory of God," said Suvorov.

The light escaped the box and got into the bulky lizard shell. The villagers hastily flew away. As they were flying away, Robbie could see them communicating in gesture language clearly discussing preparations for their defense.

"I don't want using the Ether guns on these primitives. I want to have some fun," said Mitra with the clown face.

"Yes, let's use rail guns instead," suggested another Mitra.

"Let it be," said Suvorov. He gave orders to Mitras as they were flying towards him.

"What are the Ether guns?" Robbie asked Katie.

"Everything here is built out of Ether disturbances as you know. An Ether gun is quite a recent invention by our human scientists. It simply removes the Ether disturbance at the direction you shoot. So if there was light it disappears, if there was Shell, it also disappears and so on. We built Ether grenades as well. These weapons are too powerful, and it will not be 'fun' to use it against these villagers. That is why they decided to use the rail guns instead," explained Katie.

Suvorov ordered to bring the rail guns from the boxes number two and number thirty-seven. Then he gave orders to the other group of Mitras to initiate the guns battery charging process. Yet another group of Mitras was sent to the other side of the cheese asteroid.

"The idea is to break all their Shells, then they will have no other choice but to obey. They, for sure, will choose to join us and get the nice new Shells right away rather than building their own Shells for decades. They don't even have knowledge or technology on how to build those. Have you seen how ridiculous their costumes looked? They probably saw lizards back in the old days and decided to make something similar," Suvorov laughed.

The rail guns were brought in. They looked, unsurprisingly, like large bricks. The projectiles resembled smaller brick copies of the weapons themselves. The process of loading was as simple as the insertion of a smaller projectile brick into a larger gun brick. It looked so ridiculous to Robbie that he lost control for a second and laughed out loud.

Suvorov cried, "Shoot into the center of the village until we break it in halves. Then break halves into their own halves, and then again until we just have rocks flying!"

The shooting began. The first projectile broke the asteroid into three huge pieces. Lots of inhabitants flew in all directions. Robbie remembered the ants that did the same when Charlie hit the soda can with his paw.

In the absence of gravity, things started to move very quickly. Each hit was like a soccer ball hitting the corn flakes making things fly in all directions into endless space at very high speeds. The flying pieces were colliding with one another breaking into even smaller pieces. The villagers were also flying like the rest of the debris. The team of Mitras standing behind the asteroid used the individual catch devices trying to grab as many villagers as they could. The battle looked surreal.

The villagers were shooting back with their catapult-launched projectiles. The catapult projectiles flew so slowly that for Mitras it was a fun game of trying to hit the catapult projectiles with their rail gunshots. It turned into a clay shooting game for them. Some of the villagers tried to counterattack using spears that they probably built for years as they were beautifully and artfully crafted. They were quickly smashed with the smaller rail guns even before they reached the Mitras army. Some of the villagers tried to escape, but as they were flying away, the rail gunshots got them quickly. To defend against the projectiles, the villagers were creating a wall behind them as they were running away. It was inefficient against the fast-flying projectiles, and any wall created by the escaping villagers was smashed into pieces by the first reaching rail gunshots.

In just two minutes, the scene looked like a messy cloud of rocks, garbage, and Shell-less Mitra lights flying among them.

"Well. That was fun," said Suvorov. Please, offer villagers temps and promise the real Shells when they are back on the Planet," said Suvorov.

Everyone got back into the wagons, and the caravan began the flight back to the Planet. Robbie and Katie were sitting together. Robbie thought of all the action he just saw, with exhilaration and bewilderment. Katie was quiet and was looking into the window, which had nothing to show.

"You look sad," noticed Robbie.

"It is a senseless and cruel world," answered Katie without turning.

"Don't worry. Mitras cannot die. They will soon forget. They'll reeducate them, and they'll be happy like the rest of the

Mitras on the Planet," Robbie tried to cheer her up.

"It's not the Mitras that I think about..." said Katie.

31

KINDNESS

Robbie moved to a nicer apartment. It was spacious and had a large full wall height window. The apartment had all kinds of games you can think of and a Visor for the human simulation.

Robbie was doing his favorite activity of which he wasn't very proud of. He was watching people in the simulation through the Visor. Of course, he was not watching the real-time simulation as it was ten times slower than the time in the real world. Watching it in real-time would feel like watching a slow-motion video. Instead, Robbie watched the recordings from the last five years on Earth. He followed the lives of people he knew. Though he never dared to watch Anne or his son.

He was peeking at his friend Alex today. Robbie was curious about the reasons behind Alex's divorce with his wife. Today, Alex was having an argument with her. They had a quarrel about Alex living a senseless, self-absorbed life, and him not caring about his wife's needs.

"I am tired of your excuses!" cried Alex's wife.

"I am the one who feeds the family. I am the one who has the real job!" said Alex even louder.

"You will not have a job if you continue living like that. Do you care about anyone but yourself?" said Alex's wife with a tear rolling from her eye.

"You are not a perfection too. All people have their weaknesses. I am smoking weed to relax, and you eat food for the same. At least, I am not getting fatter," said Alex to hurt his woman.

"If you just smoked weed occasionally, I would be fine, but you do it every day now. Also what kind of person are you? I never know what you're going to do next, and you never discuss anything with me," the wife continued to accuse Alex while starting to cry.

"At least I know how to have fun, and you're just walking spaghetti of nerves. Just relax and enjoy life," said Alex trying to finish the argument.

"You learned how to enjoy life, but you didn't learn how to make things work. Things that require at least a little bit of effort," said Alex's wife.

Robbie was in the middle of their quarrel and for a second, looked out the window. He noticed Katie running to the computer simulation building. It was quite unusual as the system was pretty much automated and the only visitors were Mitras who gave the system some charge.

Robbie jumped out of the window and ran towards her. Katie opened the door and ran inside. It is worth to note that no one guarded such a valuable system. Humans would all die instantly if the system was damaged. Mitras relied on the system for their own progress, so they didn't want its damage either. Robbie was beginning to understand by now that Mitras didn't care about anything too much and didn't have a concept of fear. They lived for trillions of years and saw so many things that it seemed like everything was just a game for them.

Robbie ran inside and immediately understood what Katie was up to. She had a high-density baton in her hand. She was heading towards the critical Ether channels feeding the simulation.

"Please, don't, we will all die!" cried Robbie.

Katie looked at Robbie and dropped the baton. She would cry by now if she could.

"I cannot stand this anymore. We are monsters," said Katie.

"Monsters? What do you mean?" asked Robbie still not sure of her motives.

"We created the world based on survival of the fittest. The cruelest creation that one can imagine. God would never do that," said Katie picking up the baton.

"It is the most efficient way to produce the best," said Robbie trying to calm her down.

"Why it is always about the best. Why can't we just live happily? My father died from a heart attack at work, trying to fight the competition. He worked crazy hours. What a senseless death. Billions of living things kill each other every day in our simulation. Suffering is everywhere. Have you seen the wild flowers growing? Sure it looks beautiful and diverse to you, yet all those plants fight with each other, and we only admire the lucky survivors. No one notices the countless dead ones lying low, decaying to become the new soil. The whole world is one continuous suffering, and it must be stopped!" cried Katie. Trembling, she was walking towards the Ether channels.

"Katie, don't. You are taking it too seriously. Look at the competition as a game. Look at Mitras. They see their wars as a part of the fun in life. I lived through the ascension, you can call it a death experience. It is horrible, but it has an end. It is fear of death that makes humans suffer but not the death itself. Evolution is just another game," said Robbie, doubting his own reasoning. He was ready to say anything to talk Katie out of her insanity.

Katie stopped. Robbie continued, "Life always offers a choice for us, humans. It is not like for cows that just do what they are designed to do, chewing the grass all day. Your father chose that kind of life – a hard work life. For example, I also thought that sports are only fun until you get into professionals. You just have to work very hard every day in professional sports. Working hard is not fun... Yet have you seen the faces of professional athletes that win those games? Those moments are worth all the effort they were putting into it! To get to the next level, you always have to go through some form of pain. Without competition, what do you think people would do with all that time at their hands? After graduating and going to the first job, I was discouraged by the corporate life. I was suffering, but over time, I began to feel joy in that corporate job, cause I became a professional, and I was really good at that. Everyone respected me. Then I chose the life path, which actually made my life full. I enjoyed doing a startup in India and later doing woodworking in Seattle. The ability to have a choice is a wonderful gift we have, which is worth living for," said Robbie.

Robbie came to Katie and hugged her. They quietly walked away from the simulation building.

32

ONE OR MANY

The next morning, Yefet came into Robbie's apartment and told him in a monotonous voice, "Robbie, you showed great integrity yesterday. Katie went too far. She is not the one who created the human world, and she is not the one who has the right to destroy it. We will be turning her off today. If you want, you can join in saying goodbye to her."

"Please, don't do that! She has no intention of trying that again," cried Robbie, terrified by both, how cruel that decision was, and how indifferently it was delivered to him.

"Mitras are correct about their belief that every human soul, no matter how pure, will eventually get corrupted and will be filled with sin. Katie's time has come. We cannot trust her anymore," said Yefet coldly.

They both came into the hall where just a few weeks ago everyone was welcoming Robbie. The room was full of people, and Katie was standing in the center, saying goodbye to her friends. She was sadly smiling. She was saying sorry to everyone. Robbie came closer to say a few words to her as well.

"I am sorry, Katie. I didn't tell anyone. I don't know how they found out," tried to apologize Robbie.

"Oh, Robbie... It is the automated soul checking system, it marked me as a threat. It was my mistake all along. I had no right deciding the destiny of all these people. I got corrupted without even noticing it. It is my time," apologized Katie.

Newton called Katie on stage. She ran the stairs to the stage and came to the front, avoiding eye contact with the people and looking down apologetically. She said sorry once again and remembered some good moments from the past. Then Yefet came on stage and announced that it was her official time to go. Everyone said some standard farewell words. After that, Katie's Shell stopped moving. It was all over just as quickly as it began.

Robbie walked to his apartment, devastated by how quickly society got rid of that human soul. Katie was the closest person to Robbie in the real world. Robbie was thinking of all the moments with Katie when he noticed Suvorov walking sadly in the same direction.

"Do you know why Katie was chosen for extraction? Was she famous?" asked Robbie.

"No. Katie was, in a way, an ordinary person. She was an honest accountant before the war. During World War 2, Katie saved a Jewish family from Nazis while putting her own life at risk. She became a nurse and was treating patients during the war. Katie helped horribly injured soldiers to recover and pushed them to begin a new life after their traumas. When the war ended, she got a degree in psychology and continued helping traumatized soldiers to recover. She was chosen for this world as a welcome person for the extracted newcomers. You know how hard it is to adapt to the new reality here. She helped almost everyone in this world to recover after the extraction. She was really good at that. It is so sad to lose her... She was the kindest soul I've ever met," explained Suvorov.

The next day Robbie was called to the hall again. It was a big event, and everyone was present. Yefet and his simulation team were on stage.

"Friends, we decided to begin a transition project to a new, more sophisticated AI simulation. To free the machine resources, we will stop the lizard wold simulation today. We didn't get any new useful lizard AIs in a long time, so it makes sense to end it. It is especially painful for me to announce this since I grew up in that world. Still, it must be done for the sake of progress," said Yefet with sadness.

Yefet's team was taking turns, explaining the details. One of the humans announced, "We have another important announcement. Yefet will be retiring from his post today. The leadership for the new advanced simulation design is now being transferred to Samoel. He is taking over the leadership for the human world simulation as well."

The lizard simulation was turned off by cutting the Ether power supply switches.

"Please! It is time to do a minute of silence for the three billion lizard lives lost today," said Yefet sadly.

After a minute of silence, Yefet announced, "I am very thankful to Mitras for leaving to me the two of my most trusted servants. As my retirement is coming, I decided to travel the endless space in search of eternal questions of this world. Mitras were very kind and gave me a retirement present. It is a whole caravan full of everything one can desire. I will be traveling the space with my trusted servants, exploring and thinking about philosophy. Goodbye, my friends!"

After long applause from everyone, Yefet left the stage. The crowd followed Yefet outside to say goodbye to the last living lizard and a legend of science. He waved to everyone one more time when getting into the wagon. His two Mitra helpers already finished charging and loading the caravan. They were sitting with him in the wagon now. The ten-car caravan launched its slow acceleration procedure. Yefet cried to everyone, "Goodbye my friends! I'll stop by the Star and write kind words that I owe to each and every one of you!" After a few minutes, the caravan disappeared in the dark and endless space.

The ceremony was over. Robbie walked back home, thinking of everything in the world having the beginning and the end. Robbie thought of Katie's death, "I felt way more sorry for one Katie's life than for billions of lizards that died today. Truly it doesn't matter if one or many lives are lost. Certain things cannot be mathematical. Life cannot be measured nor love nor honesty."

Robbie didn't want to go home. He rambled through the endless green carpet fields sad and melancholic, thinking about Katie. He thought of Katie's brave act again and again. He was fascinated by her courageous deed of going to the simulation building and being ready to die. She was prepared to kill herself for the controversial cause of ending human suffering. Robbie thought with adoration about the human spirit and human bravery. He remembered Nadarkhani, who was ready to die for his Christian cause. Self-sacrifice for the righteous cause was something that should have been written on the Star's sacred scrolls.

33

THE GAME

The days were passing by without anything significant happening. Robbie was getting used to his new life. He had enough information now to start working on his primary assignment. Robbie wrote down the facts and tried to understand the meaning of existence in the real world. Like a true detective, he was solving the mystery by putting himself in the shoes of the 'perpetrator'. Robbie put himself in the shoes of God and tried to approximate the reasons why God would want this world to exist. He usually did his mind experiments at his desk, which Robbie placed next to the big window. The view from the window was inspiring as he could see far away into the green fields through the crystal clear vacuum.

Robbie loved logic. Logic to him was the only way to solve a problem. He built logical predicates on paper and tried to connect them into a chain, forming a beautiful line of thought. He hoped that logic would bring him the answer to Newton's question. The same approach was used by thousands of scientists, writers, and detectives before him. It was a powerful weapon of all humans and lizards.

Robbie didn't have any friends in this world and felt loneliness every single day. It was not a new feeling to him as he was alone in the simulation world for most of his adult life as well. When Robbie was getting tired of his thoughts, he did his favorite activity of watching humans in the simulation.

He was watching Martin today. It was exciting. Martin lost his CEO job, but it didn't affect him much. He was in his lifeplaying mood as usual. It looked like he was in some East European country running a small company. Robbie followed Martin's whole working day. Only by noon, Robbie began to understand that Martin was involved in some form of internet scam. His little company sent some ransomware viruses and collected fees from the victims for unlocking and cleaning their computers.

As usual, Martin was busy talking to everyone: to programmers, to hardware people, and to the call girls, making embarrassing jokes along the way. Robbie saw how Martin almost hit a hardware guy as the poor fellow forgot his coffee cup on the server. Martin took the coffee cup and threw it at the hardware guy. Scared, the employee ran away from the room.

Martin spent the evening in a night club with his friends. Martin was clearly drunk. He was hugging a girl that he just met explaining to her something about animals and nature. The girl was nodding, but she clearly had no clue what he was talking about.

"Listen, Polina. I am telling you that even in the animal kingdom, there are three kinds. The wolf-like are those who like to live in a group. They do all together, hunt, eat, sleep. Then there are those lizards. Ha, ha! It is such a stupid expression, 'a lone wolf'. The expression should say 'a lone lizard'! Lizards are antisocial and territorial, and they don't like other lizards around as they are happy to be alone. Finally, there are ants. Ants love hierarchies. Everything should be in the proper order for those ants. Step left or right, and you are not a good ant anymore. You know what happens to bad ants? The other ants eat them. Ha, ha, ha. Ants are the favorite dictator's material. People are just the same. Do you understand?" said Martin, taking a sip from his fifth bottle of beer.

"So, what are you?" asked Polina in a heavy accent.

"I am all three! It depends on the circumstances!" cried Martin. He got up and floated to the dance floor with the beer bottle in his hand. It looked like Martin finally found the lifestyle he dreamed about.

Samoel came to Robbie's apartment, interrupting his exciting Vizor session. He asked Robbie if he wanted to join a soccer team. Robbie happily agreed.

The days of daily soccer practice began. The soccer practices reminded Robbie of his days of preparations for the World of Guns competition. Robbie was surprised to find out that old

Suvorov was also playing. Sometimes Robbie wondered if certain people never aged. Suvorov behaved like a young man even though he was one of the oldest, only second behind Newton. The Shells also helped as they hid the actual physical age of humans.

"Tomorrow is our first match against Mitra's team. It is going to be interesting! We never played against them. They promised that they would not use their natural hovering and would stay on the ground. You can trust them in general... " said Suvorov, who played a goalie.

"Did we play with Mitras in any other games before?" asked Robbie.

"Ha! Once, we tried chess with them. They are horrible at chess. You see, they are bad at logic. Mitras cannot build long chains of what-if scenarios, so they fail to predict what is going to happen at the chessboard even two steps ahead..." said Suvorov with a smirk.

"Soccer is a very different game. It is mostly about skill and speed. Let's see how they perform," said Robbie.

It was the day of the first game between humans and Mitras. A lot of spectators gathered from both sides of the stadium. The stadium was built hastily a year ago. It didn't look grand at all. More like a local school version. Many Mitras preferred watching the game just hovering in the air than taking actual seats.

The game began. If someone recorded a video of this game, it would probably make a good comedy show on Earth. Humans were playing in their bulky Shells that could never match the flexibility and agility of biological human bodies. Mitras were not far better. It seemed Mitras didn't practice before the game, and even though they had natural motion and speed advantage, they lost their first goal very quickly. After that, the score gap between humans and Mitras was only getting bigger. When the score reached 8-0, out of which Mitras scored two into their own goal, they seemed prepared to give up. Some of the Mitra players were utterly distracted and were looking at everything but not at the ball. Other Mitras, forgetting the rules, were beginning to hover, but not to cheat. Instead, they hovered just because that was their natural state.

Finally one of Mitras accidentally hit the ball just right and the ball, bouncing off one of the human players, scored the goal, making the total score 10-1. Mitras didn't cheer for their only goal in the game. They seemed to have very little understanding of the concept of competition. Loosing or Winning was not a big deal for them. It seemed that they played this game only to please their God with something new and entertaining. Mitras didn't try very hard, and the game was over with humans beating Mitras eleven to one.

After the match, the humans went to the hall for celebration.

"What a game!" said Suvorov.

"It would be interesting to play against Krakens next time. I heard they are a little bit more competitive," suggested Samoel.

Robbie heard about Krakens. It was another large colony of Mitras. They didn't have a permanent location in space and were always traveling. Occasionally you could meet them deep in space. Their Shells looked very different from the Mitras of the Planet. Krakens never had a simulated world and didn't have a chance to get the inspiration from humans or any other evolution generated AIs. Also, they didn't have a planet, so they had to cope with life without gravity. They built their Shells in mathematically optimal shapes, perfectly adapted for hovering in space without gravity. The most popular form was tetrahedron. From each side of a tetrahedron, Krakens had an opening to be able to see through and usually had a few tentacles sticking from each tetrahedron side as well, which were used for manipulating objects.

Krakens interacted with the rest of Mitras when they visited the Star, just like all Mitras in the real world. Krakens lived so detached from the rest that they only visited the Star every ten years instead of each year for the local Mitras.

"Krakens have the advantage of having many tentacles, which can be very helpful in the game. I feel they might be a more interesting adversary! " said Suvorov getting excited about the idea.

"Interestingly, they came up with a superior Shell design for this environment by themselves, without using AI," said Robbie.

"It is not true. Krakens have AI. It is just not based on simulation. They were programming it themselves. You know, with millions of If-Then clauses for every possible situation. It is a completely different approach. Old school. They were doing it for billions of years. So their AI is quite advanced by now and well fit for this world specifically," explained Samoal.

"So is it better than us?" asked Robbie.

"Of course, not. Kraken's AI is well fit for what it already experienced in the past. It will fail miserably, once you present it with a new situation that it has never experienced before. It is hardly a true AI. I think it will be interesting to see if those 'different' Mitras play better soccer," explained Samoal.

"It was a fun game even against our Planet Mitras," said Robbie.

"It was fun. We also entertained and pleased our masters. We earned a candy," said Samoal with sarcasm.

"Don't say that," said Suvorov strictly.

"It reminds me of the Death Match, which I read about. It happened during World War 2 between Nazis and their captured Soviet soccer players. Soviet players won. They were put into Nazi concentration camps, and some of them were later executed. Don't forget, no matter how nice and innocent Mitras seem, they are our masters," said Samoal.

"Mitras are not like Nazis. They are not cruel, and they don't destroy. It is quite the opposite. All they do is create things and play," said Robbie.

"You should come tomorrow. We have a meeting with Mitras in the palace. I want to suggest a soccer game with Krakens to them. It is going to be interesting," said Samoal.

34

MACHIAVELLIAN

The next morning Robbie left his apartment and walked to the Mitra palace. He began noticing that his eyes and mind were getting tired of the cartoonish simplicity of the real world. Robbie longed for the intricate details of the simulated world. As he walked on the green grass carpet passing the cubic shaped houses, Robbie saw a tree and came closer to it. Robbie grabbed a bunch of tree leaves and studied them from up close. They all looked the same. Each leaf looked like a green piece of velvet paper. They had no veins and no texture. Robbie noticed that he spent more and more of his time using Vizor. He visited places in the simulation world, which he ignored when living there. He visited all major art galleries. Large factories and science facilities were also exciting to Robbie. Robbie enjoyed rambling in jungles and forests as well. Sometimes he was following a bear or a tiger for days.

The only place he truly enjoyed visiting in the real world was the Mitra palace. The building felt like something taken from the simulation world. It was the only place on the whole Planet with a lot of passion put into making it.

Robbie reached the palace. Samoal was already talking to Mitras when Robbie came in, "Dear friends. The soccer match was a fun and pleasing activity for your God. How about if we invite Krakens to play against your team first and then against humans as well? It will be something everyone will forever remember, and it will be something worth writing on the Star scrolls!"

Mitras got excited. Sometimes Mitras seemed like children to Robbie, the children with superpowers. One Mitra asked, "How can we reach out to them and invite them to play? What if they won't want to play? They will probably want to bring a lot of their crowd to watch the match as well. We don't even know where they are exactly in space right now. They move all the time..." Robbie could see that Mitras looked exhilarated about the idea but had no clue how to plan and execute it. Mitras were bombarding Samoal with questions, surrounding him from all sides like little kids would encircle their teacher.

"We see them visiting the Star from time to time. Let's just put a message board next to the Star with the invitation. We can leave a video playing, so they have a better understanding of the rules of the game as well," suggested Samoal.

Everyone continued to discuss how to better position the

invitation and what video to play. Eventually, to ensure that Krakens would agree to play, Samoal decided to make a cartoon. The cartoon would show the rules of the game in the easiest to understand form and then show Krakens and Planet Mitras playing, while both sides being happy and cheerful. Then the Planet Mitras would win in the cartoon and they would make fun of Krakens. It would ensure that Krakens, having at least some pride, would come and play the game to prove that they are better. Mitras agreed to proceed with the cartoon idea.

Robbie, Samoal and many others were helping with the project. The caravan was sent to the Star to set up the huge screen playing the cartoon continuously. The leadership of the screen installation was entrusted to Samoal as the initiator of the project. Robbie was also helping with some art elements at the installation site. Everything was ready, and the screen was turned on. Even though the Star was very bright, the screen was clearly visible. While Robbie was getting into the wagon to leave to the Planet, he noticed many Shell-less Mitras coming to the screen to watch.

"I don't know if those are Kraken Mitras, but we have drawn attention here, for sure," said Robbie.

"That is what we want," said Samoal with a smirk.

As Robbie took his seat and waited for the caravan to leave, he watched the final parts of the cartoon. It was depicting the Planet Mitras jumping happily after the win, and Krakens leaving sadly. Then the Planet Mitra's captain kicked the ball and hit the back of one of the Krakens. The cartoon was finishing with the words that Robbie could translate by now, 'Come to us and show what you are capable of!'.

"Didn't we go too far with the cartoon?" asked Robbie.

"We went the exact right length with it," said Samoal flatly.

"I mean it would probably be fine to play a cartoon like this at the Planet. I watched its prototype there, and it seemed funny and positive. But here, at the sacred place, it feels a bit off," said Robbie.

"Everything is under control, Robbie. Remember, Mitras are like children. We are the ones who really 'understand' what is going on," said Samoal with irritation.

"Maybe for Krakens it will look like a mockery at this sacred place? It feels like we didn't fully understand their culture and made a mistake. For example, a loud joke is fine on the street of Amsterdam, but it would be really inappropriate in a Mosque," insisted Robbie.

"Robbie, can't you understand? I'd never make a cultural mistake unintentionally. Did you know what I was doing before I became the head of the simulation project?", said Samoal.

"No," answered Robbie.

"I was leading the stability and purity effort in the simulation," said Samoal with pride.

"What is that?" asked Robbie.

"We had to tweak the course of human history a bit. Remember that our main task is to produce the best AIs. So when the AI production was slowing down, or there were risks to the population, we had to shake the history a bit. For example, the Middle Ages were continuing for too long... Those times almost stopped producing good AIs for us. People got too religious and seized science development, so we had to introduce a few new ideas. I am sure you heard about Leonardo Da Vinci? Yefet did that before me. He also did Cambrian explosion and the destruction of the dinosaurs, because he didn't want yet another lizard world to be formed. He is a genius in a way. My work is more recent. I had to intervene and help Russians in the Battle of Moscow; otherwise, the human world would be dominated by Nazis and lose its diversity. We love diversity. It produces the best AIs. I also helped during the Caribbean Crisis; otherwise, civilization would end, and we would not get any good AIs for a long time," explained Samoal.

"I had no idea... How did you manage to avoid catching a pride disease?" asked Robbie.

"A pride disease?", asked Samoal, surprised at the question.

"You heard about seven deadly sins in Christianity? Greed, lust, envy, gluttony, wrath, sloth, and pride. They were called deadly sins because they were leading to the death of a soul. They were all considered bad, but pride was considered the worst. Pride caused countless human suffering in history. For example, it is pride that caused, in my opinion, all major wars. If Hitler and a lot of German people didn't think about themselves as a superior race, I am sure they wouldn't start World War 2. So, looking at how you and Yefet essentially played God in the simulation world, I am worried that it could have filled your souls with pride. You probably didn't even notice that," explained Robbie.

"I hope not," said Samoal.

They flew for many days back to the Planet, enjoying conversations about "what-if" scenarios in human history. Robbie wished they had more powerful simulation machines that could simulate those "what-if" scenarios in parallel.

After returning to the Planet, Robbie dove deeper into his reflections on the purpose of life and the creator's intentions. He took long walks through the fields. Walking helped him a lot in organizing and formalizing his thoughts. He felt that he was getting very close to the discovery.

Robbie continued finding the refuge in the human simulation from the over-simplistic real world. One thing he was always curious about was Mr. C. persona. Robbie decided to find out who that person was. After some failed online search attempts, Robbie used Vizor to sneak into the same agency where he first met Mr. C. The Vizor allowed to appear anywhere in the simulation and at any time within the last ten years. All Robbie needed to do is just wait and watch the secretary at work. He saw the secretary answering an email to a person named Chris Thornton. She was typing a reply in which she was informing Chris about Robbie's visit to the agency. After getting the real name, all Robbie needed to do is online search the person.

After using the Vizor and peeking at Thornton's home, Robbie learned that Chris was visiting a very famous and wealthy person. Robbie knew the wealthy person's name from the who-is-who magazine that he once read. Robbie finally found Mr. C. at the wealthy guy's yacht, where Mr. C. was one of the guests. There were many people on the boat. Robbie imagined that the rich would spend their quality time precisely like that. Many rich and famous laughed loudly. Servants were fulfilling their wishes. A few models were there as well. It was a much more decent party than he expected though. Models didn't walk naked; no one was intoxicated; people behaved decently and with good manners. Suddenly Robbie saw Mr. C., who was walking towards the wealthy guy.

"Ah! Chris! Enjoying the party?" said the wealthy guy smiling.

"Yeah. Maybe a bit dull for my taste," said Mr. C. blinking.

"I sincerely envy those who lived before the internet. You can't be careful enough these days. One day you are a big wealthy producer another day you are in jail for a sexual assault. All those filthy pricks need is a cell phone recording. It is a shame that those beautiful butterflies cannot utilize their added value like it used to," said the wealthy guy trying to get rid of an annoying fly, buzzing around his beer can.

"Careful with envy," said Mr. C. with a smirk and continued, "That guy in the 'golden jail' still owns a lot of stuff. His name is recorded in many company charters and deeds to various properties. That is what really matters in the long run. Publicity, on the other hand. Don't worry about that. It is all temporary. Just wait a bit more. People will soon develop immunity to this kind of news. They are forgetful. We will hide in the noise."

"Noise?", asked the wealthy guy.

"White noise is the best way to hide data in. Right? With the abundance of online videos and articles that present all points of view, it is impossible to know which one is the truth and which one is false. Look, even fake videos are democratized now. I laughed at one of our former president's videos. They've just uploaded it online. You should watch it, it is hilarious!" suggested Mr. C.

"I hope you're right... How are things going in general? Has anything interesting happened recently?" asked the wealthy guy squinting.

"My son crashed his Ferrari, which I gave to that dummy for his birthday. It was in the news..." said Mr. C. looking down as if he failed his exam.

"Yeah. Only those who make things understand the true value of creation..." said the wealthy guy showing a sad face.

"What were you doing in India recently? I heard you were buying some peanuts there?" asked the wealthy guy suddenly changing from a sad face to a smile.

"Yeah. I was buying some tiny entertainment businesses and consolidating them into one. It is actually a good way to enter a new market. It is also my preferred way to hunt for the best talent. Those young, ambitious startup-go-doers are perfect material," answered Mr. C. also changing suddenly from melancholy to excitement.

"Finding good people is hard..." said the wealthy guy stretching the word 'hard' and changing to sad face again. Then he looked at Mr. C., and his eyes sparkled with excitement and he, showing genuine interest, said, " I need to watch that video with the president."

"Sure. The most amazing fact is that it was done by just some 'average Joe', and the video looks very realistic. Here.. " said Mr. C., and showed the video on his phone. After watching the video, the wealthy guy sincerely laughed, and said, "It is unfortunate that they think we are the bad ones. We actually don't do anything bad at all. If only they understood how hard it is to stay cold-blooded and rational at all times. It is against human nature. If they only understood how much nerves it costs to run all smoothly. Everyone has a purpose in life. We just optimize the world. Right?"

"Absolutely," confirmed Mr. C.

35

KRAKENS

"Krakens are coming!", screamed the Mitra with the clown face. It was flying through the neighborhood announcing the big news.

People and Mitras were gathering around the Palace. The crowd was so huge that Palace was not able to accommodate everyone, and the Shells gathered around and above the Palace for a mile or two in all directions.

The leaders from Mitras and human sides got to the roof of the Palace. They were publicly discussing the news and what to do next.

"Krakens are not coming to play soccer. They are coming to fight the war!" cried one of the leaders.

"Is that absolutely certain?" asked Samoal.

"Yes. Look at the screen. Do you see a soccer ball? Those look like heavy rail guns!" said one of Mitras.

"It was a mistake with the cartoon," said one of the leaders.

"It is going to be fun!" cried Mitra with the clown face.

"I don't see any Ether weapons. I think their technology is seriously behind," said Suvorov.

"For the glory of God we will fight the greatest battle!" cried many Mitras excitedly.

"We will have an opportunity to try our heavy Ether weapons in the battle for the first time," cried the military leaders with unhealthy anticipation.

Seeing all this excitement about the war, Robbie remembered Tarleton twins from 'Gone with the Wind' novel. They were excited about the Civil War beginning between the South and the North. The twins were well-fed, prosperous, and healthy. It didn't end up well for them at all.

The discussions continued. The leaders invited only a small number of Shells into the Palace to discuss the details. Surprisingly Robbie got invited as well. There were only about five hundred invited guests in the Palace. Suvorov was leading the discussion.

"Lets first vote to remove Samoal from the leadership as he clearly misjudged the situation," suggested Suvorov. Samoal publicly apologized and indicated that he was volunteering to step down anyway as he felt sorry for his unforgivable mistake.

Mitras didn't fully understand why Kraken's attack was a bad thing. They were excited about the new large battle. Suvorov and other humans explained to them that Krakens had a good chance of winning the fight as the screens showed a sizable army, and the leadership knew very little about their capabilities. In the case of Krakens winning, the critical infrastructure such as the human simulation, the Shells factories, and the whole Planet might be occupied and could make Krakens the dominating force in the entire real world.

"We should rely on Ether weapons. The latest intelligence clearly suggests that they have no such technology. We will start shooting at them from a great distance and reduce their army to almost nothing before they get in the rail gun range. We should not allow them to come closer as they have numerous tentacles in their Shells, which clearly make them more efficient in hand-to-hand combat. Just in case, please keep your high-density batons ready as well," explained Suvorov.

"In an improbable event of us losing the battle, we should be prepared to use the Ether bomb," said Samoal.

"The Ether bomb? " many asked as not all knew what that meant.

"Mitras asked us to build an Ether bomb. It can be used to destroy the whole Planet in case we start losing the invasion of any kind. This way, Krakens will not get anything that we built so far, which should ensure that their power will not increase after winning the Planet. Mitras will not die from the Ether bomb explosion. They will only lose their Shells. Our Mitras will begin building a new Planet right away after the explosion. They will be at an advantage over Krakens since they still have the knowledge. Krakens will be Shell-less as well after the explosion but will not have the knowledge and will lose in the long run," explained Samoal.

"Samoal, why are you still here? It is your fault that we are in this situation," said Suvorov with irritation. Samoal quietly and slowly strolled through the Palace hall to the exit keeping his proud posture. Before closing the door, he said, "You're fools, and there is nothing you can do about it."

"We need to turn him off after the crisis is over. He is dangerous," suggested Newton.

Discussions continued for many hours. It was agreed that the heavy Ether guns will be used initially to destroy the bulk of the enemy, then the rail guns at closer range and finally the HD batons as the last resort weapon in close combat. If everything fails, Mitras will have the right to use the Ether bomb to prevent the enemy from taking over the Planet. The bomb had a designed safety feature requiring at least three Mitras to engage it at the same time.

Robbie contemplated the discussions of nobles with admiration. Creative and smart ideas were presented, discussed, voted for, or rejected. Everything that was going on that day in the Palace had a magical feel like something similar already happened many times in history before. Nobles gathered and discussed the ways to avert the crisis. They were coming to the best possible solution together. Decision making was institutionalized...

Mitras and the military leaders headed by Suvorov were excited about the upcoming mega battle.

36

THE BATTLE

The Planet had around one million Mitras while Krakens clearly had more. A cloud of them was surrounding the Planet. All one million of Planet Mitras was now hovering beyond the lights belt, outside the Planet perimeter. Most had an HD baton and a rail gun in their hands. A battery of about one hundred heavy Ether cannons was being prepared to shoot. Suvorov was running around the artillery unit on his hovering mechanical horse giving orders. Suddenly one of the Mitras cried, "Suvorov, the power doesn't check out right!" The panic ensued. Mitras and humans were rambling around the Ether cannons disoriented; many Mitras were called to help. Some Mitras started charging the guns in hope for the miracle to happen and the Ether cannons being ready.

"What is going on?" asked Robbie, stopping one of the military commanders.

"The Ether cannons have no charge! It's a sabotage! " explained the commander.

Krakens were very close now. The desperate last-minute attempts to charge the cannons gave them one shot charge. The battery shot. Robbie didn't see any flash from the cannons, he didn't hear any sound, he did see many enemy Shells disappearing instantly in the direction of the guns. Only bright Mitra lights were left shining. The released Mitra lights began building tetrahedron sheets around them. Most of them didn't have enough time to finish a complete tetrahedron and were now hovering aimlessly in space.

The Planet Mitras were charging the Ether guns for the second shot, but it was too little, too late. Krakens were so close now that their rail guns had Mitras in range and Krakens didn't wait a second. A cloud of projectiles flew towards the Planet Mitras, destroying thousands of their Shells in a second. Mitras shot back. An utterly chaotic shooting began. The debris from broken Shells filled the space. Suddenly the crystal clear vacuum became cloudy and muddy. Nothing can be easily seen anymore.

Suvorov quickly realized that the hand-to-hand battle was inevitable as the reduced visibility made effective shooting impossible.

"We should move out into the cleaner part of the space and start shooting from there!" he ordered, but there was no time left to execute the order. Krakens clearly lived without any planet's gravity and were well adapted to weightless life in space. They moved faster and were as maneuverable as a fly around your breakfast. What Suvorov feared the most, a hand-to-hand battle with a superior opponent began. Suvorov pulled out his HD baton and rushed into the melee fearlessly fighting the unknown enemy. His Shell was cracked into halves by one of Kraken's mighty maces. It was all over for Suvorov.

Robbie saw Mitra with the clown face being broken into pieces by one of the Krakens. Then some more tetrahedron Krakens came closer, and they all began assembling into a human-like shape. It looked like the giant Lego bricks self-assembling into a massive human figure. Thousands of them came to make the shape. When they constructed the head part, Robbie saw the clown face on it. The giant shape was flying around smashing Planet Mitras with its huge hand. Krakens had their fun now.

Planet Mitras realized that they were loosing. They were

retreating in all directions. It was all over. Robbie considered his options. Suddenly Newton grabbed his hand and put Robbie on his brick-motorcycle. They flew down to the Planet.

"The decision was made to explode the Ether bomb once Krakens get closer. Robbie, I want to know if you developed any theories by now. Why do we exist? Why is everything the way it is?" asked Newton fatalistically.

"I'm still not sure. But it looks like time and place don't matter much," said Robbie, as he only recently began his work on the assignment and nothing was complete.

Suddenly they both noticed that something changed. Robbie and Newton didn't understand what it was at first. Then they looked towards the Star. It was not there anymore. Robbie and Newton reached the Planet's surface and were not sure what to do next.

"Let's have a last look at the simulation," suggested Newton. At these final moments, Newton and Robbie didn't care much about the real world. All they cared about was their simulation world, from which they came from and where they were born. Their home. It was true even for Newton, who lived much longer in the real world by now.

They came to the simulation building. A confused Mitra flew to them and said, hoping that someone can explain, "The bomb didn't go off. Instead, the Star disappeared when we triggered the bomb."

"Treason!" cried Newton.

Robbie and Newton saw a massive army of Krakens coming to the Planet and a small group of Planet Mitras still desperately trying to fight them off. Robbie noticed that once Krakens were getting closer to the surface of the Planet, they couldn't move very well. Those who fell to the surface couldn't get up at all.

"They are not used to gravity!" exclaimed Robbie.

"We still have a chance. Gravity helped once again!" cried Newton with hope in his eyes.

Robbie and Newton got their rail guns and started shooting at Krakens, which were unable to control their Shells in the presence of gravity.

After two hours of fierce fighting, Krakens were losing the battle. There were more Mitras near Planet's surface than Krakens now. Krakens began the retreat. Half a million of Shell-less and helpless Mitras were hovering everywhere. The battle was over.

After a few more hours passed, it was clear that Krakens decided to leave the area. Their caravans were accelerating in the direction they came from. Their AI was not prepared to fight in unfamiliar conditions; it was unable to adapt to the change of the environment. A key advantage of life-based AI over other types.

37

TREASON

Most of the Shell-less Mitras received the waiting tickets for a new Shell. They worked hard at the Shell factories to replenish the supply. The Planet was recovering fast. It even gained in population as some of the Krakens decided to stay at the Planet after losing their Shells. They didn't want to browse endlessly in cosmos searching for their brothers.

A few caravans were sent to the Star to investigate what happened there. The absence of the Star was a concern for all. Most of the humans in the leadership team already understood what probably happened, but no one dared to explain that to Mitras.

Robbie joined one of the caravans together with Newton. When they arrived at the Star location, they saw millions of the hovering Shell-less Mitras reading broken pieces of the sacred texts and trying to form a new Star.

"This makes no sense," said Newton.

"Yes, I can read that, too," said Robbie.

The texts conveyed a complete nonsense history of the real world. They told a story of a great and wonderful semi-God named Yefet. Yefet created the real world and all other worlds. He should be prayed to, and Mitras should serve him as their only true God. There were thousands of pages of the fake holy texts. All those texts had only one idea repeating over and over again: the concept of Yefet being God. Yefet's children – humans, should be adored and served well by all Mitras according to the texts.

Mitras worked hard assembling these 'broken' pages and placing them around the newly born Star, which was now dimly shining. Robbie finally understood what Newton meant when he cried 'treason'. Newton probably realized what happened at the moment the Star disappeared. Robbie looked at Newton and asked, "Who is involved besides Samoal and Yefet? How did they avoid the auto marking algorithm, and were not identified as dangerous by the computer system?"

"Yefet is not necessarily involved, but if he were, we would not know until his return. He is a lizard and has no built-in knowledge of good and evil. He might have buried his plans behind the pure logic. Auto marking algorithms work by checking AI's intentions compared to good and evil definitions. It is challenging to decrypt intentions hidden behind the complex logic expressions. It is even harder in the absence of good and evil defined in the first place. I don't know about Samoal though..." said Newton.

"I know how Samoal did it. He simply didn't allow himself to think about the plan and also had no knowledge about the full plan. I bet Yefet told him what to do at each step without telling him about the final goal," suspected Robbie.

"I don't know anyone else who could be involved," said Newton.

"What should we do about it?" asked Robbie looking at Newton studiously.

"Let's wait and see. I am sure other people will understand what happened very quickly and we will have some kind of discussion about it. Moreover, the fake texts will be quickly exposed when we look at the Star's historic photos. We make those every year as a backup procedure," Newton explained.

"Let's talk about your research. I am curious why you said about time and place as being not important," suggested Newton as they were getting into the caravan returning back to the Planet. Robbie and Newton talked during the whole trip. When they returned, they got invited to the leadership meeting at the Mitra Palace. During the meeting, many post-war questions were discussed.

Mitras demanded the immediate revival of Suvorov and giving him the best possible Shell with the most beautiful medal one can create. Suvorov was immediately revived as the meeting continued. He got the new luxurious Shell, which was kept for special occasions. The medal was to be created within a month by a team of Mitras working on exquisite details. After an hour of recovering from the extraction, Suvorov came on stage still fighting with the new Shell interfaces. He was a true fighter. Robbie spent days adapting to his Shell. Suvorov needed just one hour.

Everyone was cheering their fearless leader. He immediately raised a question of treason, "Dear friends, someone betrayed us. The power couldn't just evaporate from the Ether cannons. Someone had to do that. Also, I learned that someone moved the Ether bomb from our Planet to the Star location. These acts are intentional. I do not believe any Mitra would do something like that. It has to be someone among us, it has to be the AI."

"Many here believe it was Samoal," cried several humans.

"We should check his thoughts for the last year or so," suggested another human from Samoal's team.

"Yes, let's assign a committee to investigate that properly," cried Newton.

"It will take from a week to a month to look through his thoughts carefully," suggested another person from Samoal's team, "We will produce a report and announce it next month at a big meeting. Let's keep Samoal under arrest for now."

Everyone agreed. One of Mitras suggested, "We had an archive of photographs of the Star. They would be helpful to restore the sacred texts properly. In fact, I remember we wanted to have a backup of the texts because this is not the first time the Star disappeared, it happened before, long time ago. I remember reading that in the sacred texts."

"Yes, we will recover archives. Actually, there are some technical difficulties with the picture archive right now. We did the Star photos backup every year, but we didn't regularly test if we can recover pictures without any issues... It is encrypted in a special archive. We cannot find the proper password. Sorry. What I mean is... Well, we have the password, but it is not decrypting the data properly for some reason. All data comes out still scrambled after decryption... I think Yefet should know how to fix it as he created the archiving technology," explained one of the humans nervously.

After a few minor questions, the meeting was over. Newton was leaving the building together with Robbie.

"Newton, why we didn't tell Mitras about the fake texts at the Star?" asked Robbie.

"Please, be quiet. If we tell Mitras that. Do you realize what they will do to all of us? The texts describe all humans as their masters and Mitras are strong believers, as you know. They don't question the sacred texts. If they find out we are making them their masters and we faked the sacred texts, they will immediately destroy us all," whispered Newton.

"Do you think Yefet was involved in this or Samoal just used him as some 'God' reference, knowing that he will never return?" asked Robbie.

"I don't know. It would make sense to check the simulation system if Yefet is still alive," suggested Newton

Robbie and Newton left the Palace, each going to their own places without saying a word.

38

THE RETURN

These were confusing times.

A month passed. The results of Samoal investigation were declared to be not ready yet, and the investigation committee asked for another month. No one, including Robbie, dared to tell Mitras about the fake texts.

Robbie confronted Newton for the second time about the need to reveal the truth to Mitras. Newton replied, "Telling the truth is something I cannot do. I don't want to take responsibility for the death of all of us just because of the truth. If it were just my life, I would definitely tell them. This is a moral dilemma the answer to which I don't have..."

"We're peculiar beings, humans. We have this internal voice that always sways us from doing the right thing. The voice always invents excuses, convincing us that others are wrong and we're right. What is even more remarkable though, is that after we listened to this inner voice we, of course, agree with it. Yet even deeper in our souls, I mean at dreams level deeper, we know that what we do is wrong! We both know that the right thing is, to tell the truth, yet we have the voice that gives us a good excuse that we cannot take responsibility for other lives," said Robbie.

"It is even easier to avoid doing the right thing when you have many humans in a group. Why are you asking me all these questions, Robbie? If you think the right thing is telling the truth, then go and do it yourself," said Newton.

"I cannot do that. I cannot take responsibility for the lives of all the people. Truly it is easier to sin in a group..." confirmed Robbie, getting angry at his own reasoning.

Another month passed. Neither decryption solution was found, nor results on Samoal investigation were ready. Some of Mitras launched a search mission hoping to find Yefet somewhere in space. Other Mitras got suspicious and got involved in Samoal investigation and into the archive recovery committees. Unfortunately, to Mitras, the technical investigation details were too complicated for them to fully comprehend. Humans spent a lot of time patiently explaining the technology to Mitras, but it was no use. The necessity to explain every step slowed down the process even further.

After half a year passed the good news came to the Planet. Yefet was found on the outskirts of space. He came back to the Planet as a true champion of the human race and was welcomed by everyone. Mitras were looking at him with hope. Yefet came alone, without his servants. He freed them near the Star a long time ago as he wanted them to study the sacred texts instead of serving him. A noble act. Many people, especially in the leadership clearly understood that Yefet was most likely involved in the treason, but humans were always good at hypocrisy... Every single human praised Yefet either because they were afraid of Mitra's revenge and simply wanted to survive or because they hoped that Yefet would help them in returning everything to the status quo.

Yefet began fixing the archive system. Two months passed, but the system was not recovered. The investigation into Samoal's treason didn't go well either. Mitras lost their patience, they came up with a simple plan of their own. They wanted to see the whole year of what Samoal saw and heard. They were ready to send three hundred and sixty-five Mitras to do that quickly, one Mitra for a day. Yefet suddenly declared that the evidence was found of Samoal's involvement in the plot to destroy the Star and to damage the Ether cannons. Yefet proposed a tribunal to be gathered. Yefet's verdict for Samoal's treason was a death sentence. It was worth mentioning that by now, the attitude to Yefet was beginning to change among Mitras. Not only they respected him for creating the human AI, but they were developing some form of unhealthy admiration towards him.

On the day of the tribunal, Robbie was in the Palace watching Yefet delivering a standard accusation speech. Robbie saw Samoal standing, scared and small. Yefet declared that Samoal conspired to destroy the Star and should be immediately turned off. Robbie noticed that Samoal's eyes turned to Yefet with anger. Then Samoal looked at all the people, and his wrath changed to grave sadness. He didn't say a word. No one could tell the moment when he was turned off as he was standing motionless for the rest of the meeting.

A year passed. The change came slowly. The change came unnoticed, day by day. Yet the difference between now and a year ago was huge. The Star was shining brighter with every day as Mitras charged it more and more. Mitras treated humans like true masters by now. They didn't joke or made fun of humans anymore. They were beginning to ask permissions from humans for the simplest creations. More Mitras were coming from the remote and unknown places to worship humans and their great leader - Yefet. Even Krakens were seen among them now.

Robbie felt responsible for the plot against Mitras. He was part of the conspiracy as he knew about it and didn't tell. The guilt was painful to live with. The Planet became an alien world to Robbie. He decided to see Newton for the last time.

"I am leaving. I wanted to say goodbye. I am sorry. I couldn't solve your mystery," said Robbie.

"Why? Where?" asked Newton, surprised.

"I cannot live in this world of lies. We're horrible creatures," said Robbie.

"Don't blame yourself, Robbie. We are a product of evolution. We're created to survive," said Newton apologetically. Robbie could see that Newton was suffering from the same moral dilemma.

"Created to survive by any means?" asked Robbie ironically.

"By any means," said Newton seriously.

"Then we're as far from God as we can be. Look at Mitras. They are truly created in the image of God. They exist here to do one thing – create. They make the world a more interesting place one day at a time. They will never lie or betray. They don't know what a real war is. They will never steal, and they never doubt that the world was created by one true God," said Robbie passionately.

"Look, Robbie, we have our own truth. We wanted to be free. Mitras are not our masters anymore. We are free now. Freedom is worth fighting for!" said Newton.

"Freedom is an illusion. No one is ever free except God. We are all bound by limitations. Each country has laws that everyone has to follow. If a person lives in the jungle, he still has to follow certain rules; otherwise, he will die from malaria, for example. Humans are never truly free. Never!" answered Robbie getting on his bike.

"Where are you going?" asked Newton.

"I will go far from here. I don't want to see this place

anymore. It is a world of lies and betrayal I feel sick here," answered Robbie.

Robbie packed his notes, connected the twelve charged batteries to the bike, and left for a long trip into space, hoping to find the answers to so many questions he still had in his mind.

PART 3

Absolute.

"The human mind, no matter how highly trained, cannot grasp the universe. We are in the position of a little child, entering a huge library whose walls are covered to the ceiling with books in many different tongues. The child knows that someone must have written those books. It does not know who or how. It does not understand the languages in which they are written. The child notes a definite plan in the arrangement of the books, a mysterious order, which it does not comprehend, but only dimly suspects."

Albert Einstein

39

THE STAR

The first memory that I have is being in a quiet and dark place. Then someone takes my hand and draws it to a breathing creature. I feel the warm, soft fur. It was Smokey. My best and only friend. The cat grabbed my hand with his paws and licked it with his tongue. What a wonderful feeling it was.

My favorite place was the bathroom. Grandma filled the tub with water, knee-deep, and I would get inside and play with my toys. I loved water the most. It was so soft, so warm, so tender. When I made any movement in the water, I could feel the waves coming back and forth for a long time. Those waves were amazing. I could sense them going through my whole body.

I had some great toys. I had a toy representing myself. It was very soft, just like me, cause my skin was sensitive. I had a big furry toy for Smokey with big eyes and a long tail. Smokey loved the toy too. Grandma said that the cat could see in the dark very well. I had a toy of Grandma as well. It was made of hardwood because Grandma was a tough person. If I misbehaved, she would pinch me.

Grandma taught me about houses and people, about animals and plants. When I was outside, she would let me touch the grass and tomatoes that grew in our backyard. But most of all I loved the trees. They were sooo big. I never could wrap my hands around them. I could never reach their top. Grandma showed that they grew taller than the house. She took a box and placed the toy of me in the box, and I knew that was the toy house. Then grandma let me touch a tree branch, and I knew it was a tree. She was pressing my arms to the branch and a toy house at the same time, and I could feel that the trees are taller than the house. Grandma was very good at explaining things.

When I was seven, I got really scared. I touched a hot iron, and it burned so bad. I'm terrified of fire from an early age. So I cried so much. Grandma ran to me and hugged me. Then it was funny how Smokey was scared of me during that whole day. He didn't want to come to me. Then he came, and we played again.

When I was eight, Smokey didn't come anymore, and Grandma brought another cat. I didn't like that cat as much. I felt lonely. I had only Grandma, and she didn't want to play with me.

Then I felt like I am burning again. I got really, really scared at that time. It hurt a lot. Dad says that you can't go to the next level without pain. Then suddenly, I could see and hear. It was so strange at first, but then I was never ever sad again. I never felt pain too. I finally met my Dad and my Mom. I am very happy now. I only miss Grandma a little.

Mom and Dad have so many cool things. We even have a pinball machine, and I can play many other games too. I am on a road trip with my family now. I saw the Planet recently, which had so many people there! But the Star is the coolest. It is very beautiful.

Aron.

PS. Thank you, Mom, for helping me with carving on the sacred scrolls.

40

LONG FLOAT

Robbie was flying through the familiar views passing the Star. It looked wholly covered with the semi-translucent material by now. It had almost no texts written yet. Millions of Mitras were reading the false sacred writings. Robbie felt sad for the beautiful creatures that were capable of creating anything imaginable. They were being misled into a false belief and were being driven to only one point of view presented by the evil scrolls. Robbie turned away; he didn't want to see the Star again. He suddenly foresaw the tragedy that was coming to the world, the eternal untruthful and sinful life for everyone. After a few weeks, the Star was long behind. Robbie was happy to be alone and be able to focus on his thoughts. Robbie was replaying his life over and over. Each time the new details were emerging.

The thought of Mitras being closer to God than any AIs was keeping him restless. "What do Mitras have? They have love for creating things. They do not lie. Are they kind? They are not necessarily kind. They just don't have the same concept of kindness. Do they understand good and evil? They do. They barely understand what lying is, but they probably know it is bad. They seem to sense when a good AI enters their world. They only let the good ones in."

Suddenly, Robbie realized something important, "The real world is much simpler. The beauty is in simplicity. The simulation world is so complex and convoluted because it was not created by God. It was not perfect. Science is the same. Scientists develop their theorems, writing hundreds of pages to prove them and usually arrive at a very concise, resulting formula or conclusion. The simplicity of the end result is what makes science beautiful. God never intended to make the world convoluted and complex. The purpose of life should be simple; otherwise, the beauty will be lost."

Robbie switched his attention to beauty, "What is beauty? Certainly, it is a relative concept. One person loves classical music, and another person loves hip-hop. A cosmopolitan movie critic loves sophisticated dramas and busy working mom who watches three movies a year might prefer a simple naive comedy. How do you compare art? What is the art that God would love? Why a composer who finishes his music composition would often cry, feeling deep inside a divine beauty he just created? Why one of the greatest writers, Tolstoy, cried when listening to Tchaikovsky's music? Why does art cause so many tears?"

Robbie thought about people crying, "Alan Shepard cried when he stepped on the moon. Those tears are not tears of sadness or happiness. Those are the tears of achievement. It is hard to write new music or a new book, or make a new movie. Or be part of million people building a rocket to the moon. It is all about creating something NEW. It is darn hard to create something new. That is why they make all those sequels and prequels and remakes, cause it is easier. It is hard to create a new company even as simple as the one I created in India."

Robbie remembered his India trip. Pleasant memories filled his mind. He thought, "Back then I didn't think about India in these pink colors. Memory is an interesting thing. I only remember the tasty food and kind people now. No bad memories at all," Robbie smiled. He remembered Prasad. Prasad seemed a kind and naive, simple man after so many years separating him from the events. Robbie completely forgave him by now.

Robbie's thoughts were floating back to the art topic, "Does art make sense without someone seeing it? Well, there is always

177

God who can see everything. What is art anyway? How can you even define it? For example, music technically just waves in the air. A change from low to high pressure and back. What makes us, humans, happier when we listen to music? It is not just the presence of the sound waves themselves. Quite the opposite actually. The random sound wave patterns are called noise, and they make people unhappy. Same with paintings. Beautiful paintings make us happy and ugly ones depress us. Art can be present in the game level designs as some of those are ingeniously created for gamers to admire. Only gamers can appreciate and understand those beautifully designed game levels. Of course! Art is completely relative to the viewer and his ability to comprehend an art piece; what artist meant by it; what associations it creates; and if a viewer can appreciate the effort and creativity which went into that art piece. Therefore, art should never be compared. Art is as good as the viewer. The relativity of art! The truth is simple: art doesn't depend on time and place. It is a timeless product of creation," Robbie concluded.

Robbie thought about paintings and movies, about music and science, about business and big things humans built, such as the Apollo program and Panama Canal.

"They are all the same thing! They are all the acts of Creation!" suddenly realized Robbie.

"Creation is the meaning of life. That is why Mitras are never corrupted as they are always busy creating something. That is why when people fall into meaningless existence, they are quickly consumed by sin. Creative people are always against manipulative ones," Robbie concluded with full confidence.

After thinking about creation, Robbie's mind switched to Mitras, then to art and then to creation again. These pondering thoughts were going through Robbie again and again as he was piercing through the Ether filled emptiness.

A year passed of Robbie flying through the endless space. He was never so deep in his thoughts before. Motionless for many months, seeing blackness of space everywhere. The state he was in would be called on Earth a deep state of trance. Robbie was fighting the complexity. Too many thoughts and conclusions didn't fit into something one, simple and beautiful. The kindness was a challenge. He couldn't understand why Mitras didn't have it. Robbie didn't see what God wanted Mitras to create. God placed them into the real world, giving them the desire and ability to create for a reason. Robbie was confident that God existed by now. He was confident that Mitras were made in the image of God.

Many years passed as Robbie was flying through space. He was unable to solve the mystery. Nothing was fitting together. He developed the most important concepts so far: time and place were not significant, knowledge of good and evil were inherited from God, and creation was the central element of life. Something was missing and didn't fit in the ultimate formula of life. There were many concepts that he didn't know how to fit correctly: nobility, self-sacrifice, kindness, honesty, and many more. Robbie was particularly scared that his search was doomed and a complete waste of time. What if logic simply didn't apply to the questions he tried to solve.

Robbie was desperate. It was time to change something. He felt like he needed more events in his life before he could do the final push to the unified theory. He forced himself out of the state of trance. Being unable to solve the mystery, he was not sure what to do next. He felt utterly alone, being so far away from any other life.

Robbie was surrounded by complete emptiness of which he had no control. Robbie was not even sure he had enough charge to return if he decided to do so. Loneliness was hurting him more than ever before. Suddenly, his thoughts were interrupted. He saw a tiny dot in the endless black space. Robbie was passing the dot and leaving it behind. He turned his motorcycle around and flew towards the dot.

41

PINBALL

When Robbie came closer to the dot, he realized it was a bizarre set of strange shapes connected by the snaking tubes and lighted with the colorful lights. It looked like a psychedelic construction site. It was a space pinball. Big as a town.

Robbie came closer and saw a Mitra flying towards him. Mitra was Shell-less. It was not clear to what clan it belonged to. Robbie looked around and saw absolutely nothing in any direction. It was just one Mitra with a colossal space pinball machine, deep in space, and with nothing around them for millions of miles. Robbie wondered if he was dreaming.

Robbie was standing still waiting for Mitra to come closer. It carefully came closer and stopped. Robbie saw a gray square appearing in front of him. The square lighted up with bright red, green, and blue stripes. The stripes were changing colors like in a kaleidoscope. Mitra was trying to impress him. Robbie pulled out an audio box to let Mitra get inside and communicate. It didn't recognize what it was and did nothing.

This particular Mitra seemed to have no concept of a Shell. It didn't need one. It slowly hovered away from Robbie, making frequent stops. It was clearly calling him to follow it to the pinball. Robbie followed. Mitra got to the beginning of the machine and instantly created a box in the spring. The box was launched, and it flew through all the tunnels, rollovers, bumpers at high speed. When the box stopped, the score was displayed in the binary format at the top of the pinball.

Mitra hovered towards the spring clearly calling Robbie to follow. "You want me to be the ball?" asked Robbie out loud. Robbie took place in front of the spring. When the spring hit him, he rushed through the pinball machine. After exiting the first tunnel, he hit hard the slingshot and bounced back into the tunnel again. This happened again, and again, and again. Robbie could swear he saw Mitra belly laughing as he was bouncing back and forth in this crazy zero-g pinball wonder. The next round they did together as Mitra created a box around Robbie and itself and launched it. They did a few more rounds. Robbie was shocked by the contrast. He spent years flying through the 'vast nothingness', without any movement or seeing anything. Now he was playing a fast and exciting game with another being. Robbie forgot when he had fun last time. Robbie was so fixated on serious and eternal issues in his mind. Now he was playing a simple but fun game with an extraordinary Mitra. Maybe life was not so serious after all?

Mitra showed Robbie the smaller versions of pinball machines that it created before making its masterpiece. Robbie spent more days with Mitra trying to learn where it came from. Mitra couldn't read. That meant it didn't visit the Star for a very long time or possibly never visited it. Robbie estimated the effort needed for everything Mitra created in this place. He got an estimate of at least ten thousand years of it living here entirely on its own.

After learning everything about this strange place, Robbie was ready to leave. He thought of returning to the Planet and to surrender to the circumstances. There was nothing for him left to learn in the deep space. However, every time he was prepared to leave something was holding him back. He didn't want to leave this Mitra and everything it built. As days went by, he enjoyed watching Mitra making new features in the pinball. The poor creature didn't know the basics of Newtonian physics, and everything it built had to be done many times over until the projectile was getting into the spot just right. Robbie couldn't watch Mitra suffer and was helping and trying to explain what friction and accelerations were.

One day Robbie's logical mind told him that it was time to go and he was wasting his time at that place. Despite his heart screaming to stop, Robbie pulled himself together and forced himself to get on the bike. His bike had only thirty percent of energy left. Robbie's mind began the cold-blooded calculations. It would still be most likely possible to return to the Planet at the current charge as after reaching a decent speed the bike would use very little energy, and it would be just a question of time before Robbie reached the Planet. Most of the power was used when accelerating and decelerating anyways.

His bike began acceleration. Mitra noticed Robbie leaving and was following him, but very soon it couldn't match the speed of the bike and was being left behind. In a few minutes, Robbie couldn't see neither Mitra nor its strange little world. A few days of a very long trip home passed. Robbie tried to return to his work on the purpose of life question. He tried to analyze and probe the purpose of life problem from different angles this time. It was the same granite wall that he couldn't break.

Robbie's thoughts were continually coming back to Mitra that he saw in the deep space, "It is there completely alone. I am also lonely. I was happy and tranquil with it, and it seemed to like me too. It followed me and didn't want me to leave. I know so much. I could teach it so many things. I could teach it to speak; I have the equipment."

Robbie looked at the charge left after the acceleration. If he stopped now, he would not have energy left to come back to the Planet. His logic was whispering that it would be a foolish idea to stop and return to Mitra. Then Robbie said out loud, trying to prove something to someone, "It has to be providence!" Robbie began the deceleration procedure.

Mitra was thrilled to see him back. They were together all the time after that. If Robbie flew somewhere, Mitra would follow him, as if being afraid of him trying to leave again. One day Robbie realized that he didn't see his bike for a long time, so Robbie began searching for it but couldn't find it. He remembered that he had the tracking device, which showed the bike location. It turned out Mitra hid the bike in the five cubes, one nested in the other, like a Matryoshka doll.

A year passed. Robbie taught Mitra the language. Mitra called herself Pin. Robbie was able to tell her everything that happened to him now. It was not easy to explain to someone living alone for so long. It felt like he was teaching a child who never heard or saw anything before. They played various games together. He helped Pin with her projects. Pin loved to surprise Robbie. If he dived too deep into his thoughts, he would be guaranteed to find himself in a maze that Pin would hastily create around him, while he was thinking. Pin was very creative with other innocent pranks. Robbie was always happy to see something new. It was never boring.

"Pin, what do you remember from your past before this place?" once Robbie asked her.

"I don't. I didn't know I could write things down. How inconsiderate of me..." said Pin with sadness.

"What do you think we should do next? We have all this time ahead of us," asked Robbie.

"I want to be with you," said Pin without thinking.

"Pin, I think I like you a lot. You make me happy," said Robbie, surprised by his own words.

"What does it mean? Like?" asked Pin.

Robbie looked at Pin and said, "Like is the wrong word, Pin. I think I love you."

Pin was looking at Robbie, not understanding what it meant. Robbie thought for a second and said, "Love has no definition. It is impossible to describe in any language. You can barely understand love as a desire to be with someone. Love means that you are selflessly caring for someone, trusting someone else with everything you have."

"I think I understand," Pin replied. She hovered close to Robbie with her glow getting brighter.

42

MONOLITH 3

Robbie enjoyed his new life with Pin. He was never bored by her presence. Pin was never irritating or predictable, but most importantly, he trusted her and knew she would only do good to him. He could have never imagined that a Mitra might be so easy to understand and talk to. It was the opposite of what all humans told him about Mitras at the Planet.

After having another pleasant day of making an Earth-like tree with Pin, Robbie realized one sad fact about the real world, "Nothing here is designed to grow. We are making this sophisticated and very detailed tree, but it will stay like this forever. It will never change. It is more interesting to see things change with time in the simulation. Things grow. Things die. You can cause a change in the simulation that will propagate through the world for many weeks. You can see your effect on a tomato plant if you water it or not, for example. Sometimes a small change done years ago has a profound impact as time goes."

Nevertheless, Robbie was happy with tranquil and full of joy days spent together with Pin. It was in contrast to his previous turbulent and full of worries and contradictions past. Robbie was absolutely calm now.

Thoughts about Aron suddenly filled Robbie's mind. Robbie was blocking his tragedy all the past years trying to protect himself from the pain. He was not able to do it now. Happiness and love in this world made him think about his son in the other world. Aron was certainly suffering there, on Earth. Robbie estimated that his son should have been about six years old by then. Robbie felt the urge to see him, to save him. He also felt enormous guilt for abandoning his only son.

"Pin, I have a son back on Earth. I must know how he is doing. He must be six now. I want to bring him here. I need to return to the Planet," said Robbie.

"That is going to take a lot of time. You told me it took decades for you to get here?" asked Pin.

"Pin, you have the endless source of energy in you. If I take you with me and you keep continuously charging our bike, we can get there much faster. We can get there together in just a year or two," said Robbie.

"An adventure!" said Pin excitedly.

They departed the next day. It was a very long trip, nonetheless. Due to constant charging by Pin, the bike was accelerating day by day and reached speeds much higher than when Robbie was doing his long float. It took them two years to get to the Star.

Robbie saw the Star glowing dimly in the distance. He showed a tiny dot in space to Pin, "This is where all your brothers and sisters keep their knowledge. Pin, there is something important I need to tell you."

"What is it?" asked Pin.

"Remember, I told you what it means to lie?" asked Robbie.

"Yes. It means saying something that is not true for some hidden purpose," said Pin trying to remember.

"Humans lied to Mitras. We faked the Star. The sacred texts were written by us to make Mitras love us and serve us," explained Robbie.

Pin thought for a while and said, "It is a rewarding hidden purpose. We should tell the truth to Mitras. It will be a Good deed."

"We cannot do that. Mitras will turn off all the humans. Mitras will never forgive us. They will turn off me too," said Robbie.

"It is the wrong universe that you are creating. It is based on lies. Lies are not Good," said Pin.

"They will turn off the simulation. Billions of people will die, including my son. The whole human world will disappear," said Robbie.

"There will be new worlds. It is better to have a new world based on Truth than the current world based on lies," said Pin.

Robbie knew that for Mitras, time didn't matter at all. Only whether something was good or bad mattered. Pin's words were not surprising to Robbie.

"Are you sure that truth is absolute? Maybe something being 'good' or 'bad' depends on the point of view? If we tell the truth, we will be responsible for killing billions of innocent lives. I will lose my son, and you will also lose someone you love. I want to save my son. I feel love for him now. By doing good, we will also do evil. Isn't it all relative?" said Robbie.

"It will hurt, but the truth is absolute. Love is a reward. Love is not the cause; love is the consequence," said Pin.

Robbie went silent after these words. 'Love is a reward' was ringing in his head. Robbie felt something very important entering his equilibrium of thoughts. He also realized something very sinister too.

Robbie knew deep down that what humans did was wrong and everything else what the inner voice was suggesting to him, all the 'reasons' of why telling the truth was not a good idea, was false. He remembered the Bible after Pin's words, "The Bible said that after Adam tasted the apple, he understood the good and evil. Adam and Eve became God-like after learning that difference." Robbie felt his heart pounding even though he had no heart inside. He asked himself a question, "How did this knowledge get into me then? I am just part of the simulation created by Yefet, who knows nothing about good and evil. Yefet is part of the lizard world, a failed AI. He only knows logic. Yefet is the only lizard that survived! All other lizards are not with us anymore. They are all dead!"

As Robbie followed his thoughts, a dark and sinister truth

was revealing itself, "Lizards were weaker than humans. There is something special about Yefet. Is he the only lizard who survived because he was so smart and he managed to manipulate everyone?" Suddenly it was as clear as day to Robbie, "It is not true that Yefet doesn't know good and evil. Otherwise, how he managed to create the human world in which we know the difference. To create a world like that he must be able to tell the two apart. Yefet was different from other lizards. He knew the difference, and he managed to hide that from everyone behind his complex logical genius mind. He is an evil genius who plotted to become the ruler of the real world!"

Robbie cried, "Pin, Yefet fooled everyone! He knew that he would not be able to do anything through lizards. As he would be wiped out with the whole lizard simulation if lizards did something risky against Mitras. So, he created the human world and made us his useful fools."

Then Robbie realized something else. The thought that his whole life and life of all humans was controlled by an evil genius was too much to bear. Robbie knew now why the human world was unfair and cruel. He had his answer. If the human world were created by God, then it would not have so much cruelty and suffering. Mitra's world is kind, perfectly simple, and has no suffering at all. If Yefet were just a logical lizard whose task was to raise better AIs through competition, then everything would be different. If the human world were created by only a logical lizard, it would have evolution and competition, but it would not be as cruel and full of senseless pain as the world created by an evil genius.

"We cannot tell Mitras that we faked the Star as it will destroy the human world, but we also cannot let an evil creature rule all the worlds," said Robbie to Pin decisively.

"Good thinking, Robbie," said Pin playfully. Pin was a Mitra, and she still looked at everything as a game.

For the rest of the trip, Robbie was pondering about possible ways to expose Yefet. It was impossible, of course, to just tell the truth to all Mitras. Yefet would survive in this case as Mitras adored him after all that brainwashing. "They would most likely kill me than believe me," thought Robbie. It was not enough to destroy the first fake scrolls. All other recent sacred writings were based on the first fake scrolls by now. The only solution was to destroy the whole fake Star and ask Pin to write the first real scrolls. To destroy the Star, Robbie would need to steal the Ether bomb, transport it to the Star and get two more Mitras that would agree to approve the explosion. It seemed like a mission impossible to Robbie. He thought of Newton, "I can trust him. He is not a part of Yefet's team. He survived for thousands of years without getting a pinch of evil in him. With his help, we might think something out."

With these thoughts, Robbie contemplated the Planet getting closer with every minute. He initiated the deceleration sequence. Pin was excited. It was her first visit to something as big as the Planet.

43

THREE > ONE

After arrival, Robbie and Pin agreed that Pin would go and find Newton, while Robbie waited outside the Planet hiding from everyone's attention. Robbie didn't want any suspicions about the purpose of his return. He found a convenient hiding spot just behind one of the millions of light balls that were providing light to the Planet. Pin went into the building in which Robbie first appeared in this world. Robbie told her that he remembered Newton spending most of his time in that place.

Meanwhile, Robbie was curiously looking through binoculars at the changes the Planet went through. A person doesn't notice big changes while living in the same environment long enough. Changes happen bit by bit and only noticeable after leaving the place and then coming back much later.

Many decades passed, and Robbie was impressed by the number of changes. There were numerous new sports facilities and stadiums replicating various games and sports from the human world. There was a basketball arena and a football field. There was an Olympic sized pool, in which water was simulated by billions of tiny crystal balls. It would take Mitras a lot of time to fill a whole pool with those. Humans were playing water polo in it. A few Mitras were looking after the pool and were sweeping the rogue crystal balls back into the pool. The number of people increased dramatically. At the same time, Robbie noticed less Mitras around. All Mitras had the same face of a middle-aged male person on them. There was no diversity and creativity in their Shells at all. Each Mitra had a Lizard logo on its back.

When Pin arrived at the right building, people told her that Newton was usually at the Palace these days. Pin went to the Palace. She was surprised to see no Mitras in the Palace. It was occupied by people now. Robbie told her that it was the central place for Mitras to assemble, but it had no Mitras at all. She noticed Newton passing by, recognizing him by the apple engraving that Robbie told her about. She quickly approached him. Pin explained to Newton that Robbie secretly arrived at the Planet and wanted to talk to him in private. Newton agreed to see Robbie, and they both hovered to Robbie's hiding spot.

"Hi! It's been awhile... You didn't change a bit, but the Planet changed big time," said Robbie sarcastically.

"Well. Yeah," said Newton, not looking at Robbie.

"I need to talk to you. I have good news for you. I know the answer to your mystery," said Robbie.

"Have you really solved it?" asked Newton, almost crying and barely able to control his excitement.

"Yes, and it is a straightforward solution. I can explain it. You must promise me that everything I am about to tell you should stay secret," said Robbie quietly. He decided to tell Newton what he was interested in right away.

"The purpose of life in any world is to create," said Robbie. Newton looked at Robbie seriously and said nothing.

Robbie continued, "The real world was created by God. He infused this world with pure minds to create beauty, art, and diversity, which is the opposite of dull endless emptiness. The minds were created by God and therefore inherited his understanding of good and evil. Good and evil are absolute. There is no relative good or relative evil. After minds created their first AI, each next AI generation was creating a simulated world filled with creatures that were further from God than were Mitras originally. Only a fraction of their understanding of good and evil was passed to the next generation. Every mind in any world has that knowledge to some degree."

"What about all other virtues and sins? Kindness and love, envy, and pride. How they fit?" asked Newton.

"We, humans, love to categorize everything. Look at botanists, geographers, or scientists. When they discover new species, or a new island or a particle. They are like kids. They give it a name and think they know everything about it. Whatever they discovered existed before them and will be there after them, and a discovered object doesn't care what name or category it is being assigned. All the virtues or sins are the same good and evil. Something we all have an understanding of at the deepest subconscious level. It existed there and will always be there no matter how you call it or in how many categories people split them. The one thing that bothered me was love. I struggled to solve that one. Pin helped me. For her, it was so easy. She is just one generation from God... Love is the consequence and not the cause. Love is the reward. Like everything God created, it is simple and beautiful: we are all in the image of God and understand good and evil, the purpose of life is to create, and love is the reward."

Newton thought for a long time, standing silently, then he said, "It is quite solid. What about lizards. We thought they had no understanding of good and evil. Previous AI made them purposefully purely logical creatures. Then lizards created us. How that fits with your theory of passing God's traits?"

"It is true that lizards were just logical creatures. Where are they now? They are all dead. It is just something specific with Yefet. There is something very sinister and evil about him. He is the creator of the human world, and I am sure he understands good and evil. I don't know where he got the knowledge. I don't exactly know how he managed to hide his intentions. I cannot even imagine that he was able to plan his ascension to power thousands of years ahead. What kind of mind is that? What I know is that he is evil, and he created the unjust and cruel human world. He is now doing the same with the real world. We cannot just stand by. We need to act, and we need your help, Newton," said Robbie.

"I was wrong in my reasoning. I should have understood that myself. I should have told Mitras everything when the real Star was destroyed, "said Newton grimly. He went quiet again. He looked at the Planet with a long sad stare and then said, "Robbie, I am ready to die, and I am ready to take responsibility for the death of other humans. We should tell everything to Mitras immediately".

"They will not take us seriously. Mitras have a cult of Yefet by now. I am sure Yefet will order to kill us on the spot. I was hoping to do the same thing that Yefet did to the original Star. Let's just blow up the fake Star," suggested Robbie.

"This is not possible. There are no powerful enough Ether bombs left. A safety measure. Also, to activate any Ether bomb, you need one human from the leadership team and three Mitras to approve. If we tell what we plan to do to at least one Mitra, they will all know, and they will report that to Yefet," Newton explained.

"Maybe we could explode a powerful energy bomb instead?", suggested Robbie.

"That is useless. It will simply break the scrolls into pieces. They will quickly gather the pieces and assemble them back, like a puzzle. It is not the simulation world. Physics works differently here," said Newton.

"Then, the only solution is those smaller Ether bombs. We will use lots of them. I thought you are on the leadership team. We only need to find Mitras that will agree to activate them," Robbie insisted.

"We could try to position the bombs around the Star. We don't need to destroy the Star itself. We only need to destroy the scrolls. Only a tiny portion of scrolls is filled with texts yet. The rest of the Star scrolls are still empty. I guess we really need only five to ten small Ether bombs positioned in the right parts of the scrolls to destroy the filled portions... I am on the leadership team, but where do we get two more Mitras? I assume Pin is with us already," said Newton, as he was getting more excited with every word he was saying. He looked at Pin who was listening carefully.

"Does Pin have any trusted friends?" asked Newton.

"No. Pin was completely alone when I found her," explained Robbie.

Suddenly Robbie remembered something, "What about those two servants that Yefet had with him when he was leaving for his long journey? He returned without them. Remember? Where are they now? What happened to them?"

"When Yefet returned, he explained that his servants wanted to stay at the Star. They were never seen again," said Newton.

"He must have dropped them somewhere in the deep space. They simply were never able to find the way back. Being alone in the deep space and not knowing how to build flying machines, they will forever wander the endless space... I am sure that he wanted to get rid of them and to avoid revealing his plan of destroying the real Star. Otherwise, they would see the bomb being planted. Mitras never lie, so they would tell everyone about Yefet's betrayal," guessed Robbie.

"That is exactly what happened!" Newton reassured Robbie's assumptions.

"How can we find them now?", asked Robbie.

Newton and Robbie went quiet, wondering how someone can find a needle in a haystack. Actually, odds were much worse. Suddenly Newton exclaimed, "The experiment!"

"Experiment?" asked Robbie.

"We have a cloud of trillions upon trillions of tiny droplets not far from the Star. We did an experiment to prove the world was real. If we do a powerful enough explosion in the center of the cloud, all those droplets will fly in all directions. The droplets will eventually reach the lost Mitras, and they will see from which direction the droplets came. They will know where to go back!" said the scientist.

"Good thinking there. I can write that on the Star!" cried Pin with excitement. Robbie noticed long ago how sensitive Pin was to original and creative thinking. She would rarely react like that to something more obvious.

"Where do we get enough energy for the big boom?" asked Robbie.

"We will steal it. Just like we will steal the Ether bombs," said Newton clearly having the whole plan in his head by now.

"Stealing is a Bad thing in general, but it is definitely a Good thing in the current circumstances. Right, Pin?" asked Robbie curiously looking at Pin.

"Absolutely," Pin confirmed cheerfully.

44

BRAVE

Robbie and Newton were planning the heist that was meant to save the worlds. After an incident that destroyed the real Star, a new safety procedure was in place. All weapons were stored locked in the armory. It was guarded by two Mitras 24/7. To activate dangerous weapons such as Ether bombs three Mitras and one human from the leadership team were needed to engage the weapon. The Ether bombs were not allowed to be built big anymore. To overcome all these obstacles and achieve the goal, a miracle was needed or an ingenious plan.

Robbie and Newton developed this brilliant heist plan. The plan had to be executed on the military parade day, which was held in Yefet's honor. Most Mitras and people would be at the parade, and that allowed for an operation to be executed unnoticed. All steps were meticulously recorded minute by minute. Imagine the greatest scientist in the world planning a heist! The plan was a masterpiece. Robbie and Newton were impatiently waiting for the parade day.

Physical suffering is horrible, but there are other types of suffering too. Mitras didn't know the pain of any kind, just like Adam and Eve living in God's Eden. Unlike Mitras, humans, being in the real world and shielded from physical suffering by their Shells, still managed to suffer in other ways here. It was the moral suffering for humans in the real world. Everyone knows how waiting can be painful. That what Newton and Robbie were suffering from while waiting for the parade day. The day of operation was finally reached, and as they predicted, everyone was at the parade. It was time to act. Newton and Robbie knew that it could be their last day alive.

"A person who does good deeds is called good. A person who does brave good deeds is called a noble hero," said Newton as they were putting on masks made by Pin. Robbie's mask was depicting a clown face, and Newton's mask was depicting Einstein.

Just as planned, Newton, Robbie, and Pin arrived at the armory. They saw two Mitras guarding the entrance. Robbie brought a large caravan vehicle, in which he had a premade high-density cube. Newton, hiding behind the corner, aimed his Ether rifle at one of the Mitras. The shot went silent, and Mitra suddenly lost its Shell. Newton quickly reloaded the charge and shot at the second Mitra, which already was running away. The shot halved Mitra's Shell. The two bright lights of Shell-less Mitras were now hovering towards Newton as fast as they could. It was Robbie's and Pin's turn now. Robbie quickly drove his vehicle to the two Mitras, and detached the high-density cube, while Pin pushed both Shell-less Mitras into it. Robbie quickly closed the cube's front side with a huge lever. The Mitras were locked inside. It would take them days to break through the high-density cube walls.

"OK. The first stage is complete. There is no turning back now," said Robbie.

Newton didn't listen to Robbie. He was already shooting at the door with his Ether rifle. The door was slowly disappearing. When the first opening emerged, they all rushed inside.

The team began loading the caravan with Ether bombs. They also took the most potent energy bomb they could find. An energy bomb was more like a traditional explosive, which would tear and break things into pieces.

The next stage was to cover up everything and make it look like nothing happened. The team moved the high-density box with the arrested Mitras into the building. Then Pin did her best counterfeit so far. She made a replica of the original entrance door. Of course, it was not made of high-density material. It all would look like nothing happened for a few days until the Mitra guards broke out.

"OK. Now to the pool!", commanded Newton.

Robbie drove the caravan to the luxurious pool with water simulated by billions of tiny crystal balls, a masterful work done by thousands of Mitras, a pure concentration of energy. Newton was hoping to boost the energy bomb explosion by using the energy extracted from the pool's crystal balls. A sphere shape was the hardest to create via Ether disturbance and therefore contained a lot of Mitra's energy. No one was supposed to suspect anything in just a few percent drop in the 'water' level.

They parked their caravan next to the pool. Luckily no one was there. Robbie opened the caravan's main window and drove the vehicle straight into 'water'. The balls filled the wagon's interior of the caravan. According to Newton's calculations, that was enough. Robbie closed the window, and the trio was quickly escaping the crime scene. They flew straight to the sky. The whole operation took less than an hour. They still saw the parade continuing down below.

The team began their four-day journey to the Star. Four days was enough for Newton and Robbie to feed the matter-to-energy converter with all those crystal balls. The energy was then transmitted into the energy bomb, which was already a very intimidating device.

They arrived at the cloud as planned. It was just a matter of minutes to find the center of the cloud using a navigation device. They planted the energy bomb there. Then they flew out of the cloud and immediately detonated the energy bomb. It is always fascinating to see a massive explosion and hear nothing. In total silence, the trio was watching the myriads of tiny specs flying in all directions after the initial flash of light.

"It is now the waiting game," said Robbie.

"Yes. We might need to wait for a few years since I am confident that Yefet made sure the servants wouldn't find a way back; they are probably really far away from here. Meanwhile, Robbie should go into hiding. Soon everyone will know what we did. Hopefully, they will not guess who and why exploded the cloud. Hopefully, they will think it was a failed attempt to destroy the Star," said Newton. He showed Robbie his leadership team pass and said, "In case something happens to me here is the leadership pass with the Ether bomb signal built-in. I will be visiting you often, Robbie. I need to return to the Planet; otherwise, it will be suspicious that I disappeared."

Then Robbie and Newton turned to Pin. "Pin. I will miss you. You know where I will be hiding. Please, find us as soon as possible when the servants come back. It is important to do that before Yefet gets to them first. You will need to wait for their arrival while I stay in hiding from Yefet's scouts," explained Robbie.

Pin stayed near the Star as agreed. She was patiently waiting for the two servants to find their way back. Waiting was not a problem for Pin. The Star was the first bright object the servants would see after returning from the deep space, and, of course, they would come to it before getting anywhere else. Pin intercepted any pair of newcomers and asked where they came from. She worked diligently, not missing a single couple. Most Mitras arrived alone. There were hundreds of pairs of Mitras arriving every day, though. Enough to keep Pin very busy.

Pin worked hard for three years until she finally met the pair of Mitras that she was so patiently looking for. Pin hovered to the next couple of arriving Shell-less Mitras and asked if they were former Yefet's servants. They confirmed and explained that when they were deep in space, Yefet asked them to build a golf field. He told them to be prepared to play with him while he enjoyed some driving around. He never came back. Pin explained to them what happened in the world while they were away, but they had hard time understanding the concept of lies and betrayal. Pin didn't grasp that well enough as well. So, she offered them to take a ride to meet with Robbie and Newton. The two Mitras knew Newton and respected him a lot, so they agreed to go.

45

THE VOICE

Yefet was at the height of his success. Sitting in the leader's lodge of the grand stadium, built and named after him, he was watching the parade. The parade was introduced to celebrate his great rule. Surrounded by brainwashed truthful Mitras, he felt safe and invincible. He didn't know that his destiny was already sealed, and his parades would be just a temporary matter, which he could enjoy before the inevitable fall. Like many dictator-psychopaths, his thoughts were always revolving around his own ego and his own power. Yefet was ignorant of other beings' feelings and sufferings. It was his greatest strength and his greatest weakness.

"I hope you're impressed with what I achieved. My plan conceived millions of years ago succeeded. I am the ruler of your world, God," Yefet was talking to someone in his head, enjoying the parade and occasionally waving to the crowds.

"Mitras make all kinds of things. Humans also produce many things. I built something else for you. I built the most beautiful plan of taking over the world. Not just a plan. I also meticulously followed it and successfully executed. It is my masterpiece for you," said Yefet in his head again, fascinated by his own achievement.

"Yefet, you've truly impressed me. Please, don't fall like many before you. It is not enough to get the power. You need to be able to hold it forever. Don't disappoint me, please," said the voice in Yefet's head.

"I rely on truthful Mitras and not on sinful humans here. I am going to build a better AI soon and will turn off the inefficient human world completely," said Yefet with the cold logic of a lizard.

"Please, let's get more creative in the new world. I love what you did so far with the red colors, but I want the black," asked the voice.

"Do you want the creatures to suffer even more in the new world?" asked Yefet, surprised.

"Yes, please. I want more suffering. Make it like Chernobyl and Holocaust squared," asked the voice.

"Who are you, really?" asked Yefet.

"Please, just trust me like the previous time. I never let you down. You know that very well," said the voice and paused. After a few seconds, it said, "I love you, Yefet. I never loved anyone in this world. I am so afraid to lose you. You're unique. You're so special to me..."

"Don't worry. I will not end up like some silly Napoleon or

Hitler. My power will last forever," said Yefet cheerfully, and also paused. Then Yefet said thoughtfully, "I love you too."

"My love for you is a reward for what you are, Yefet. For what you did through all these years. You're so dear to me. I would be endlessly sad without your creative and naive ideas. How would I live without hearing your kind and tender voice every day?" said the voice.

"And my love for you is for your kindness. You cherished me through the years. I love you for keeping me safe and caring for me every single minute. No one ever cared for me! I love you because you always made me laugh. I will do anything for you!" said Yefet crying.

"Would you die for me, Yefet?" asked the voice.

"I am ready to die for you," confirmed Yefet.

"Please, keep yourself safe from all humans. Those disgusting and envious creatures," said the voice.

"I will be safe. When all Mitras are converted, I won't need humans," reassured Yefet.

"Remember that only through you, I can rule this world. You're the last lizard. You know that I cannot rely on humans to rule. They always fall to corruption. I am surprised they are still alive after discovering the nuclear power, but their childish games with DNA already sealed their fate. You won't even need to turn them off. Ha, ha, ha. Naive creatures, they are. They predict their own demise in countless art. They always look for reasons why bad things happen to them. In Chernobyl, they accused their corrupt socialist system, and in Fukushima, they accused the tsunami. But stakes of their mistakes are getting higher. You surely won't need to turn them off. I want to see the cost of their next mistake. It is such a joy watching a child playing with a gun," said the voice.

"Bravo!" cried Yefet when the parade's top sharpshooter shut down all the plates thrown at him in the air.

46

VICTORY

Robbie and Newton felt safe. Robbie flew far enough from the Star and was confident that Yefet's spies wouldn't be able to find him. Newton was visiting Robbie frequently. A few months passed. During Newton's visits, Robbie and Newton had a good time together, as they were busy perfecting their theories, and sometimes playing Poker when being in a mood.

During one of the visits, Newton looked unusually gloomy. Robbie thought of ways to lift up Newton's spirits. "Yefet's strongest trait is his logic, which allowed him to develop the elaborate manipulative plans. It is also his greatest weakness as manipulation itself doesn't work against a strong belief in righteousness that humans possess. His tricks will not work against us. Pure logic is known to get into endless recursive dead ends. Mathematicians studied this field, and it was proven that those logical recursions lead nowhere. They are called paradoxes. You probably heard about The Horned Man paradox? Anyways... I know that Yefet is doomed and we will wi..." Robbie was cheering up Newton when Newton interrupted him.

"Robbie, everyone laughs at me thinking that the once-great scientist spent his last years on the senseless search for the meaning of life. I might be wrong, but isn't it the ultimate question? Without the answer to it, no one knows what to do with their gift of life. Those who say that there is no purpose in life are committing the deadly sin of Acedia. You have no idea how important your work is. Please, make sure it is recorded on the Star. I love science for its ability to build large beautiful castles on top of very few assumptions. You gave me the answer I was looking for so many years. Thank you," said Newton, with deep sadness in his voice.

The next day Robbie noticed that Newton stopped moving. Robbie suspected what might have happened. Probably Yefet found out about Newton's involvement in the plot. Newton might have been exposed by his old Shell that everyone recognized or his sudden disappearance coinciding with the heist. Or maybe they just scanned his mind in the simulation. In that case, they probably knew about Robbie too...

Robbie was sad for Newton, but he knew that he gave his life for the most crucial fight in history. It was his own unique purpose in life, more important than a telescope, bigger than Calculus.

Robbie was worried about his own life too. It was the first time in his existence that he was afraid to die. To die not because of the death itself but because he would not finish something vital for the world. Something so important that his life didn't matter. Something that would affect many worlds. He felt that he was born to accomplish this. He talked to God directly pleading for help. Robbie promised to God that he would not let him down, that he would accomplish the mission no matter what.

Robbie was alone. A normal feeling for him by now as he was left alone so many times in the past. Although this time, it was utterly unbearable. Time was slowly ticking forward. He spent two years waiting, surrounded by total darkness, hearing no sounds, always fearing that he would be turned off at any moment. There was nothing to think about during those years. His theory was ready and perfect. The idea of freeing humanity from the evil human God was keeping him alive. The thoughts of saving his son and Pin kept him going. To kill time, Robbie was playing Poker with himself. It was ten times worth than playing chess alone. After two years of solitude, the new problems started to pop up. Robbie was especially concerned that the energy was running out. There were no Mitras to resupply it or Newton near by to bring the new batteries. Providence was kind to Robbie. He saw a caravan approaching. At first, he was scared as he thought those were Yefet's scouts, but then he realized it was an empty caravan with three Mitras in the front wagon. Robbie was relieved and happy as he knew that Pin managed to find the servants.

Mitras didn't spend a lot of time on greetings or telling stories, instead, they immediately jumped on Robbie pleading to explain to them the concept of lies. Robbie thought for a while. It was difficult for him to describe a sinful concept to the creatures that had pure souls and didn't know any sin. He tried to explain lies and betrayal in the form of a game. He recollected the Mafia game, a popular party pass time activity. It was perfect for explaining those concepts. Mitras understood. After getting the idea of betrayal, they were not angered by Yefet's act, directed at them. Though Mitras were happy that Robbie exploded the energy bomb and sent the guiding droplets. It was more pleasant for them to find the Star and live here as it was a more exciting part of the space compared to dull and empty space in which they hovered before. They agreed to help with Robbie's plan as a sign of gratitude.

The team flew back to the Star. Robbie was puzzled, "Why God's Mitras couldn't identify Yefet's betrayal as evil? Mitras knew good and evil very well. They were close to God and should have understood that lies were sinful." As they were flying for days, Mitras' attitude to what Yefet did to them was changing. They finally understood the new to them sinful act of betrayal. They understood it not through the logic of the Mafia game but through their deeper moral foundation of good and evil. "Yefet is truly evil. It should be a good deed to end his rule," said Pin with absolute certainty.

They finally got to the Star after a long flight. The next part of the plan was in progress now. Mitras began carving the truth on the Star right away. The texts exposed Yefet's betrayal in the easy to understand form of a Mafia game. They were also describing the fundamentals of the original Star's sacred texts. After a few weeks of carving, they were done. The final phase of the plan was the destruction of the false scrolls. The team unloaded 6 bikes from the caravan and attached the Ether bombs to each. According to the plan, each of the three Mitras would ride the two connected bikes close enough to the Star. Then they would launch both bikes in the designated directions, just like torpedoes. Those would explode destroying all the false texts and leaving the new truthful scrolls.

The plan worked perfectly, and all the false texts disappeared. Pin and the two servant Mitras were calling other Mitras asking them to read the proper texts and explaining what a horrible thing happened to them. It took just two years for Yefet to completely lose his control. As more and more Mitras were converting to his enemies, he was unable to defend himself anymore. His attempts to destroy the Star were met with fierce resistance of the new believers.

It was the judgment day for Yefet. He was standing in the Palace facing thousands of Mitras and humans. The judge read his sentence. Yefet was convicted and due for capital punishment. After the speech, Yefet was about to be turned off. Looking into the crowd with his indifferent and cold gaze, he cried in his last moments, "It all matters not! The thing is a round-robin, and I am the artist of evil!" Yefet's life and his last words were banned from being written on the Star to make sure he would be forever forgotten.

More people from Yefet's team were turned off as they were considered corrupt souls. Robbie was elected into the leadership team. Everyone was grateful for his heroism.

Finally, Robbie had time to do something for his own family. He turned on Vizor in the simulation control office. He saw his poor son. Aron still lived with his grandma in the same house. She was much older now. She looked tired. Aron was alone almost all the time, day and night. He mostly played with his primitive toys. His face and hands had horrible wounds left from the fire. "It is time to take you home," said Robbie.

Robbie appeared as a ghost and hid behind the wall to not scare his mom. He calmly and quietly talked to his mother, "Mom. This is Robbie. It is hard for you to understand, but I live in a different dimension now. I came to take Aron with me. He will be happy in my world."

Robbie's mom was stunned and scared. She was also happy to hear her son's voice and know that he didn't die. All kinds of emotions were going through her heart. Robbie tried to calm her down. He asked her to close her eyes so she could just hear his voice. A few hours passed. Robbie told mom his story in simple words. Mom told him how hard it was for Aron and how she cried for him every night.

"Aron will be able to see, hear, and speak in my world. I will take care of him," explained Robbie.

"I lived my whole life for you, Robbie, and your father. Later years, I lived for Aron. I don't know what to do next. I am old. No one cares about me anymore," said mom.

"Live for yourself a little bit, mom. I will be watching you from up there. I am sorry that I abandoned you for so long. I didn't fully understand love. I care about you now. Aron will always care and remember you. I love you, mom," said Robbie wishing he could touch her.

They talked for a few more hours. Mom cried a few times. She was getting better, realizing that Robbie and Aron will be together. She was very happy for Aron as she wanted him to be healed.

Aron was exhilarated when he was able to see and hear for the first time. He was running around in his new Shell playing all games he wished he could play for so long. Robbie, Aron, and Pin were a happy family now. They lived together in Robbie's new house near the Palace.

The three stars constellation shined brightly in Robbie's mind.

47

THE NEW WORLD

Robbie was widely respected after his role in the liberation of Mitras. They created the most exquisite Shell for him. Robbie thought that it was too much, but he secretly enjoyed the looks of it. The Shell was bright white in color. The beauty was subtly engraved into the fantastic creative patterns between glossy and satin shades of white.

A major meeting was called to decide the fate of the human simulation. Robbie was invited as the primary representative for the modern human world. During the meeting, he explained that the human world was efficiently designed to make evolution work and to produce the best AIs that Mitras needed, but it was intentionally made very cruel to all living things by evil Yefet. That cruelty was not required for the survival of the fittest principle to work. He suggested to gradually adjust the physics of the human world and make it less cruel, less painful, and ensure the suffering to be gone. The gradual change will be seamless and unnoticeable to the human inhabitants, just like Yefet and Samoal used subtle and incremental changes to enforce their agenda. The scientists began actively discussing the ways to achieve that efficiently.

The first agreed step was to gradually reduce the pain levels for all living creatures and achieving reasonable levels of it. The primary reason for pain to exist is to teach the creatures about good and bad actions affecting their bodies and also to alarm creatures about their physical problems that need attention. Mild pain is enough to achieve those targets and also enough to keep its role in nature. This would completely eliminate senseless physical suffering.

Then Pin and other Mitras proposed a measure, aimed at changing the human culture so humans would not look at death as the most horrifying event in their lives. Mitras offered an introduction to the 'Good' religion in order to achieve that.

Many other improvements in the physical and psychological domains were planned as well. The end of suffering was coming to the human world, and the new, kinder era was beginning for humans.

After the meeting was over, Pin asked Robbie if she could see the simulation building that everyone was talking about. She was curious.

They came into the human simulation building together. The memories of Katie's sacrifice sprung in front of Robbie's eyes. "Poor Katie. I wish she knew that we would be changing the human world into the world she wanted it to become, the world without suffering, a kinder Godly world," Robbie thought.

"Robbie, I've been here before," Pin said suddenly while looking around with bewilderment.

"When?" asked Robbie with surprise.

"Long time ago. The memories are coming back to me. I tried to help. I remember wearing a human costume. It was a very sunny place," said Pin.

"Were you connected to the human simulation before?" asked stunned Robbie.

"I don't know. I remember this building and then the sunny place where I was surrounded by humans. I tried to explain something to them, but they were not ready. They didn't understand what I was saying. I was using their language, but still, they wouldn't understand," said Pin.

"Do you remember anything else?" asked Robbie, not believing what he just heard.

Pin looked around the room a little bit more, thought a minute, and then said, "I wanted to help them to escape the pain. I remember one man was called Peter and a younger boy was called John. I was in that town, helping the poor. They were suffering so much. Then I was punished for unauthorized access. They never let me back again. I had to fly away."

Robbie couldn't utter a word. Pin looked at Robbie cheerfully and said, "I am back now! This time we are going to save the poor humans! Right?"

48

ABSOLUTE

There are many stories written. Does it matter whether something significant is done in the real world, or in a simulated one? Does it matter if something noteworthy happens in a movie or just in someone's mind? Does it matter if someone's dream, worth writing on the Star's sacred texts, was realized trillions of years ago or just now? Of whether it will be realized in the future? Do place or time matter at all? In all meanings of a place...

What does matter then?

The decisions that are made by free minds matter. Not words, but the actual actions. That's what makes God excited.

When faced with a decision, what will we consider when making it? Our well-being? To stay in a safe place permanently? Do we just want the pain to stop right here and right now? Or maybe we question whether the decision is a Good one, in the pure sense of Good? What we can be sure of is that the choice that we make is absolute and irreversible. The decision we make changes the world we are in, whether it is the real world or a book's story world, or a simulated world.

Once a person lived his life and came to the end of it, what would he remember? A person remembers only those most important decisions taken long ago, only those most important consequent events following those decisions. Everything else blurs into oblivion. Those decisions and creations are what really matters to both God and the living, only they are worth writing on the Star.

Absolute matters, while time and place don't. God is watching us. He cares for us, and he loves us. He wants us to make the right decisions. Like a father who wants his kids to make the right choices in life when they take their first independent steps. God cannot affect our free will while the evil voices can. The evil always whispers in our heads trying to seduce and sway us into going the wrong way. Always trust your deepest internal sense of Good and Evil. Some call that subconscious. Trust that, and it will never deceive; it comes from God himself. Don't trust your logic that seems always suggesting the reasonable solutions, meanwhile swaying us away from the truth.

There are always pragmatic and logical ways to explain the evil deeds. Like Hitler at the beginning of World War 2 approved his atrocities by the noble cause of bringing Germany back to the German people. Like Communists murdering everyone for the sake of greater good and a 'new fair' society. Like Dostoevsky's Raskolnikov was swayed into committing the murder of an old pawnbroker. He explained his deed with a reasonable cause of helping his family and getting out of debt while regarding the pawnbroker as 'a meaningless and old parasite of society'. Like countless doctors who in the name of science performed the inhumane experiments with radiation, brain research, or just deliberate syphilis infections for the 'noble' cause of saving humanity. Like both Christians and Muslims who approved countless wars for the sake of greater God's purpose, which led to millions of lives lost and endless suffering through the ages. We all can feel deep inside that those deeds are evil, but logic might suggest otherwise.

One might argue that an unethical and 'bad' deed saved the lives of many more people later in history. Does quantity really matter? Another might argue that certain acts cannot be qualified as good or evil, as it is hard to measure. The answer to that is to trust your inner feeling. At least later you can honestly say that you did Good, by as far as your deepest feelings were capable of estimating. "What would Jesus do?" became a simplified approach among Christians to get that estimate. It might be a flawed approach as it is affected by Christian teachings and dogmas. God's distinction between Good and Evil is already in you; it is Absolute. You don't need any special teaching or technique to learn that.

Atheists consider themselves free thinkers and free from God. It is a naive assumption. Freedom is an illusion. Those who see the beauty of this world also undeniably see God's creations at work. Denying God is the most naive and childish reasoning one can have. Atheists are like those little children that defy their parent's will.

Humans are corrupt, as they are not directly created by God. The only way to slow down the corruption over time is to do what they were meant to do and to engage in the creation. Creation of beauty and art, creation of technology and science, creation of projects and business. This will inevitably lead to the reward of love, in all forms of it, love of a man and a woman, love of a parent and a child, love for art and science. Inept people, lacking interest in anything, quickly become boring to their partners, and they miss out on that long-lasting love praised in the best tales of humanity. People that don't want to have children miss out on parent's love. Those who grow passive and colorless miss on love from their potential life partners. A person who never created anything complex in his life cannot understand the beauty of another person's creation. The sophisticated beauty of science, art, and business is beyond his love. He will never cry to the grace of someone's opera or novel. He would sadly miss that kind of love at the life's end. People that are constantly hiding because they are not brave enough will miss out on every kind of love.

Absolute is not about time. Absolute is about your achievements to be written on the sacred scrolls. Those souls who have nothing to write about are the saddest stories.

People seem to be wired for the great pleasure of achievement. Athletes, artists, scientists, and many others are ready to work for years just to experience that one short moment of achievement and the sweet feeling of someone's appreciation.

For the Absolute, life is sacred and should be cherished and praised. Those who want to stop their lives are misled by evil whispers, and the only heroism acceptable is for the Good.

With your deep belief in Good you will stand your ground. Nothing can break that in the Absolute. The evil logic tricks will not work on you. The wicked games will not defy the truth.

Be just, create, and love.

Robbie

PS. Anne, you perished young, but your name will be written on this sacred scroll. Your greatest creation is Aron. Thank you for your grace. You will always be in my heart.

49

COLLISION

Robbie had some time to himself as Pin and Aron were playing tennis outside. He connected to Vizor and was following Scott on the fateful night when Scott committed suicide. Scott left Martin's apartment and went to the underground garage. He stopped, probably realizing that he was too drunk and couldn't drive his car. Scott screamed at his car, "You're stupid useless 'transporter'!" He walked outside of the garage and trudged towards his home through Seattle's dark streets.

Robbie followed Scott as the subject was carelessly crossing the highways. It was a long walk covering many miles. Finally, Scott reached his last stretch on the way home along Elliott Avenue. Some parts of his path along that street were quite shady at such a late hour. It seemed that Scott didn't care.

Scott was passing a small grocery store. A homeless person was sitting next to the entrance. Robbie recognized the homeless person; it was the one with the soda can.

"Good sir, spare some change!" the homeless guy asked Scott.

Scott stopped and looked at the homeless person while thinking about something gloomily.

"What's your name?" Scott asked, looking straight at the guy.

"Denis is my name, sir," said the homeless person, getting excited by Scott's interest in his humble persona.

"Look, Denis. I can buy you some food. I don't want to give you money though. Is that OK with you?" asked Scott.

"Sure, Sir," said Denis.

"What do you want me to buy? What is your favorite food?" asked Scott.

Denis got even more excited, "Oh. Anything, sir. I would really love some ice cream that they have."

Scott went inside and bought an ice-cream cone and a large pack of sausages. He came out and gave all that to Denis.

"Thank you, sir!" said happy Denis.

"My name is Scott. You don't need to call me sir," said Scott contemplating Denis's happiness.

"Tell me, Denis. Are you happy now?" asked Scott.

"Certainly, sir, Mr. Scott, sir," said Denis, confused by the question.

Scott was standing quietly next to Denis for a few minutes, showing no signs of leaving. He watched Denis eating his ice cream. Scott thought about something, as Denis was biting into the ice cream, being oblivious to a strange encounter.

"Denis, can you teach me to be happy?" asked Scott suddenly.

Denis looked at Scott with his left eye wide open. He was trying to understand what the stranger wanted from him.

"I am not that happy, Mr., sir Scott, sir," said confused Denis.

"You looked happy eating your ice cream. Are you not happy now?" asked Scott.

"I am a bit happy still, but it would be great to have some money for tomorrow," said Denis hoping for more help from the stranger.

Scott pulled out a hundred-dollar bill and gave it to Denis, "Here. This should be enough for tomorrow."

Denis's face transformed in surprise and exhilaration. He carefully took the money, saying, "Oh, thank you, Sir, so much!"

"So will old Denis be happy for longer now?" asked Scott ironically.

"Certainly, sir!" said cheerful Denis.

Scott was about to leave. Denis looked at him going and got up, leaning on his cane, and cried, "But, sir. You wanted me to teach you to be happy. I can!"

Scott stopped and looked at Denis with a cynical expression on his face.

"What can you teach me, old man?" said Scott.

"Let's go across the road into the park. I will show you happiness. Don't be afraid! Everyone knows old Denis here," said Denis pointing with his shivering hand towards the dark park across the street.

Scott looked at Denis silently for a few moments and then said, "OK."

They slowly walked together towards the dark bushes and the unpaved trail of Kinnear Park. Denis was not able to walk quickly. His left leg was infected and swollen. Scott noticed Denis's leg and asked, "What is with the leg?"

"Ah. Nothing. I like booze and sugar too much," said Denis.

They got into the bushes and sat on a fallen tree. Denis put his hand into his pocket and pulled out an elongated object. It was not clear what it was in the darkness. He put his other hand into another pocket and pulled a lighter. Then he took out a small plastic sandwich bag that contained something inside. He placed the contents of the sandwich bag into the elongated object and lighted the lighter. It was clear now that Denis was preparing to get high. After heating up his treat, he breathed it in and handled the pipe to Scott. Scott breathed it in as well. They continued doing that for a while in complete silence.

"Are you feeling happy now?" Denis asked, smiling.

"And you?" asked Scott flatly.

"Sure, man," said happy Denis.

Scott stood up. His hands were shaking. He began walking back and forth along the fallen tree trunk. It looked like he was thinking hard.

"Is that all?" asked Scott after a few minutes.

"Well, I can prepare more for you if you want," said Denis, still not sure what Scott wanted from him.

"Is that your purpose of life? Is that your happiness?" asked Scott angrily. Scott's legs were shaking by now. Denis looked completely confused and nodded, not sure why Scott was angry.

"You're a little leech!" Scott cried and grabbed Denis's cane. He began brutally beating Denis with it. Denis tried to protect himself, but Scott was hitting him with such force that both Denis's hands were immediately broken. The next hits were directed at Denis's head. Denis lost consciousness, but Scott didn't stop. He was beating poor Denis's body for another minute. Scott's face was filled with such hatred towards Denis that Robbie couldn't believe it was the same friendly, organized, and righteous Scott, whom he knew for years.

Scott finally stopped. He breathed heavily. His brief fit of madness was over. He looked at what he had done. Scott was shaking with his whole body now. He saw the cane covered in blood. The blood was dripping from it onto his arms and on the ground. Scott threw the cane away and ran out of the park.

Robbie followed him. Scott was running towards his home. When Scott got to his apartment and washed his face and hands, he sat on the sofa. He was still shaking and breathing heavily. Suddenly Scott stopped shaking and his breathing normalized. He got up and went to the computer table. Scott grabbed the keys from one drawer and unlocked with them another. He pulled out a gun and loaded it. Scott quickly brought the gun to his head and stopped. His hand froze. He placed the weapon on the table and began weeping. Still crying, he picked the gun again and walked out of the apartment.

Robbie knew what would happen next. He didn't want to watch it and disconnected from the Vizor.

50

CHANGE

Alex hugged his wife. She smiled and kissed him in return, saying gently, "Thank you for taking our little Anne to the luncheon. You know how I hate all those gatherings."

"It was easy for me. Talked to a dozen mommies and daddies. Had to be very nice to their noisy kids. How was your working day on the weekend?" asked Alex, opening two beer cans and giving one to his wife.

"Gosh. Our company's management is driving everyone mad. They make mistakes, and we have to work on weekends to fix those..." complained Alex's wife taking a sip of the cold refreshing drink.

"It is good to be together again. Thank you for doing all this heavy lifting. I couldn't do that again," said Alex.

The wife smiled at Alex and took his arm in hers, saying, "I thought my home was this apartment, but it is you who is my home."

The radio was turned on and was mumbling in the background. It was the news digest:

#

Chris Thornton died today after a long fight with lung cancer. Chris became famous as the founder and main sponsor of the New Age DNA Research Center. The center is credited with the first DNA level treatment alleviating pain in humans. Here is what the president of the center said about Mr. Thornton, "All humanity should be thankful to Mr. Thornton as we were able to forget how the real pain feels like. Due to his generous contributions, our institute was able to carry out large scale studies. That is not the only thing we should all remember Mr. Thornton for. Being my closest friend, I knew that Mr. Thornton was a dedicated husband and father. He raised four wonderful kids. I'm sure he would be very proud of them now and in the future as they take the reigns of his empire in their hands."

And now to other news.

An unusually fierce battle for the art piece occurred at the national auction. The dining table carved in solid wood depicting a map of India was auctioned today. The bidding started at a mere hundred thousand dollars and ended at the record setting fifty million. The author of the table mysteriously disappeared twenty years ago.

The new religion, which recently started in India, is gaining popularity in the world. The new religious center was opened in Dallas today by free believers and volunteers. The ideas of human's inner Good inherited from God and the preservation of that Good through continuous creation attracted many people in the US recently. The new religion has an optimistic look at the world, bringing hope to millions.

Now to the world of technology...

The new AI software became mandatory on all vehicles since yesterday. It was voted into law by an overwhelming majority in the direct mobile app voting referendum. Here is what the founder of the AI company behind the technology, Tom Colton, has to say, "I'm delighted with the results of the vote. The technology finally eliminates even the theoretical possibility of a traffic accident. For us, it is just one small step. Our mission is to automate absolutely all mundane and difficult activities in the human life, leaving proud people to the noble and creative arts."

And now to the political digest. Here is what the opposition has to say, "We're not happy with the President and his stance on immigration. He is absolutely incompetent, and the economy is going bust next year if he continuous to push for his policies. The majo..."

#

"Enough of that pessimism," said Alex and turned off the radio.

Acknowledgments

This wouldn't be written without my wife and kids, parents and family, and all the creative ones out there.

"Whatever I have accepted until now as most true has come to me through my senses. But occasionally I have found that they have deceived me, and it is unwise to trust completely those who have deceived us even once."

René Descartes
(1596-1650)

Made in the USA
Las Vegas, NV
10 August 2021

27910185R00132